ISBN-13: 9798599831273
ISBN-10: 1477123456

Cover design by: April Boehme
Library of Congress Control Number: 2018675309
Printed in the United States of America

www.jeanestelle.com

There are so many people I want to thank. There are so many who believed in me, and told me that I could do anything. First and foremost I would like to thank April who designed and painted the cover! Thank you, thank you, thank you!!

Allison, a very special Birch, in our village of Birches who took the time to read every new chapter I sent her way. She gave me honest feedback and encouraged me to keep going, to keep writing.

A BIG thank you to the beta readers who loved this story and pushed me to publish! My only hope is that you, the readers, love it as much as they have!

Lastly, my family. Jean Estelle is a dedication to my Mother, and Grandmother, with whom I share part of name. I hope she, and those I've lost since, are looking down proudly. To my daughters who are watching, this shows you that you can do anything that you set your mind to. You are my reason for everything that I do. Kylie, Sienna, you are my world. And lastly, my husband Eric. You have been my rock through this whole thing. I couldn't have done any of this without you. I love you!

Contents

Prologue

The room is spinning. I can feel the throbbing on my face where she hit me. Breathe Juniper. Though my head is cloudy, I can hear every droplet of water that hits the floor. My senses are in overdrive. If Jaila thinks she's won because she found me out, she has another thing coming. I won't give anything, or anyone up. *She will not break me*. I'm a lot stronger then she gives me credit for. She stares at me now, I assume to scare me.

"You don't intimidate me Jaila. You don't scare me!" She grabes ahold of my chin - searing pain shoots across my face and down my neck. I'm forced to look at her.

"You know, you keep saying that. Something though, something tells me that you will break soon. I will find what will break you, and you will talk. Everyone has something to protect, someone they can't lose. *Everyone* always caves in the end."

She releases my chin, my head flying to the right. I can feel the enforcers breath on my neck sending shivers down my spine. My head was so fucked I didn't even hear him come in, jerking away at his touch.

Chapter One

One Year Earlier

I was so nervous that my palms were sweating profusely. This always happens to me when I'm nervous, and I hated it. I kept wiping them on my jeans attempting to dry them, to no avail. They were dripping with sweat only a few seconds later.

I have never been so nervous in my life as I am right now. Today was one of the two times a year every seventeen-year-old was sent packing. How fucking awesome is *that*? Your parents love you. They care for you for seventeen years. Then? Then you're thrown out like yesterday's garbage to fend for yourself. No turning back, no help, all alone, no matter what, with no choice in the matter. It's what the council came to as law, so there is nothing anyone can do but obey.

It's all I've been thinking about all day. Well, months really. It wasn't real for me until I woke up this morning. I didn't – or should I say, I refused to let myself dwell on the inevitable like the rest of my friends. All they kept talking about was how they were so happy to be getting out on their own, and away from their parents. I just didn't understand it. Not one bit. I mean, if you chose to leave, and that's what you wanted, then that would be one thing. But forcing us to go and banning us until we pass, if we pass? No. I didn't like that one bit. We were only good enough for the compound if we could contribute to it. If not, then you were taking up space, using precious resources without giving something in return. And that my friends, that could not be tolerated.

The only one of my friends who was even remotely scared, was my friend Tish. She hadn't been taking it all that well. I was no help to her either, because I was just as terrified. I couldn't understand why we had to be separated from our families for six months with no visitation allowed, no leaving Discovery allowed. All alone with nothing, and no one but each other...

Well, that's not *entirely* true. The council provides you with a dorm, provides you with food, and provides you with clothing for the first six months out on your own.

The catch you ask?

The catch is if you do not find a job, a way to contribute back to the compound, or pass your chosen class, you are thrown out of the compound. If you are lucky enough to survive the radiation poisoning, you were never allowed to see your family again. You were never allowed back into the compound, or allowed to speak to anyone inside the compound ever again. They forget you ever existed, and only use you to scare others into subordination. One less mouth to feed, and you instill fear into the populace to control them in one fell swoop.

Win-win right?

What could possibly go wrong, right??

That was the way of this world though. Be controlled, killed, or deformed by the radiation above us. To me, being thrown out into the radiation, well, that was a fate far worse then death. Having to live outside, cut off from everything you have ever known, at the very real risk of death or deformity? All of this, because the so called "leaders" of this compound felt that if you couldn't hack it in six months, you are not fit to live in "their" society. If you fail, you are an embarrassment to the compound. This compound could never suffer from failure. The council simply wouldn't allow it. Like they have anyone to impress... If there were any other underground compounds, one would think that we would have found them by now. And not for nothing, If I discovered this compound being the leader of a different compound, I wouldn't trust them at all knowing what I know. I can only imagine the things that I will learn about them... That thought alone turns my stomach. One day, I will change things. One day, things will be different.

I have always hated the way things were done, but really nobody has much of a choice. There was a great war three hundred years ago. Humankind nearly caused our own extinction. It was the war to end all wars. Those who survived the nuclear radiation either died a slow agonizing death, were lucky enough to be underground, or close enough to the nukes going off that they died instantly. No one remembers who used the first nukes, or if they do, they are choosing not to say.

I used to have nightmares of dying that way, once I learned how the radiation killed you. It was either instantaneous, or slow and agonizing. Sometimes, sometimes I could imagine the cackling of my skin burning in those dreams. I was afraid to tell my mother that I began to have those dreams again, as the time counted closer to the day I had to leave. I didn't need her to worry about me even more than I knew she was going to. There was no need to add to it.

The people who thought the world was going to end during the war had built underground bunkers. Some even built their homes underground meant to withstand a nuclear attack, sustaining them for years to come. Sustain to the point where some people had UV lights set up, growing vegetables and leafy greens. Although it's only been during the last hundred years or so that we've been successful in growing fruit, but, more on that later. The reason for the war has been lost to time, or it's been deliberately hidden from us. The only reason we have been able to survive is because of the stories that have been passed down through the generations by word of mouth. It's no matter though, all we have now is this compound.

The compound. Where to begin? It started out as individual bunkers, that the first generation of the people who lived underground built out of fear. But as time passed, people found each other through radios and other means. They connected through the bunkers. Some were huge, some were small, and some were like towers going deep underground. Over time, it became a small city that gradually grew into what it is today. Then again, I really only have books and pictures to compare it to. I've never seen a real city, or even taken a real fresh breath of air...

I often think of what it was like before. I daydream of what of it was like before the war destroyed everything. I dream of what it was like before the nukes. It must have been something to just be able to breathe fresh air, to smell a fresh wildflower in a meadow...To feel the cool air breeze across your skin...

One thing I have always wanted to see was the night sky for myself. From pictures, I've seen the stars. I've seen sunsets and sunrises too. But to experience something like that in person? That would take my breath away. Things that seemed so trivial and so insignificant to humans before, and now? Now they just seem so unreachable... An impossible dream that will never come to fruition. Like the feel of the sun against my skin, or the cool ocean breeze through my hair... If I close my eyes and concentrate, I can almost see it, almost sense it, almost feel it calling to me...

I hear my mom come in, which pulls me from my reverie. I take a deep breath in to gather my own thoughts, exhaling a deep breath out to calm my nerves.

"Honey, you are going to be fine." My mother says to me as she embraces me in a hug. I hug her back. It may be a little too tightly out of fear that I might not be able to do it again, as she flinched from it. Some would call me irrational, but nothing is in here. You could disappear in an instant, and that would be that. Especially if you were one of the 'little replaceable people.'

I burn into memory the smell of her jet-black hair. Her hair always smelled of strawberries. The way she looked as she smiled right before she hugged me. The way that her eyes crinkle on the sides as she smiles. God how I am going to miss her.

After a moment, I pull back and look at her. My emotions were running wild, and were all over the place. Since I woke up this morning, I could feel the gloom. I felt a sadness like I would never see her again. It was a feeling that I did not like, nor could I shake. I knew I had to pull it together. If not for me, then for my mother.

"Mom, this is insane! Why do all of the parents agree to send their children away at seventeen? Why *must* we leave?" I ask this as the emotion runs thick in my voice. I knew why, but I still could not wrap my head around it. My mother looked at me with tears filling her eyes and I almost feel bad. I know she doesn't want to send me away, but it is the law. No matter how stupid the law might be.

My mother places her hands on my shoulders as she looks around to make sure no one is listening before she speaks. Why would she look around like that? There is no one here but us?

Right?

"Jun-" she says so low that I can just barely make it out. "Do I think this is cruel? Yes, but everyone has to go through it if they want to live safely in the compound. I have never shown you the people that survived the radiation, who are banished to live in it..." She says the last part like she is drifting away to a memory, her eyes staring off into nothing. "It is truly terrifying, especially for those who survive the radiation... That is why your father and I have been coaching and training you for what is to come, since you could comprehend it. You will do fine my strong, beautiful, wise daughter. You were born to succeed, for that I have no doubt." She says full of confidence. I wish I had that same confidence in myself...

I know she is trying to make me feel better, but I have a knot in my stomach that just will not go away. I can *feel* the panic spreading through my body. It is an overwhelmingly paralyzing feeling, and it scares me to death. Just then, another thought hits me. "How do you know what the people outside look like? If no one ever goes out, how do you know people have survived?" She looks at me concerned, almost fighting within herself. I know that right then, she is keeping something from me...

"Mom?!"

"Honey, right now I cannot tell you how I know that. Just know that it is horrible." She says, a sadness etched in her voice. I decide to drop the subject with her, at least for now. The enforcers will be here soon, and I do not want these last moments with my mother tainted.

I grab hold of her hands as I look into her eyes. What if I fail? What if I never see you again? Wh-. My mother places her hands on either side of my face, searching my eyes. When she does this, I swear that she can see right through me.

"Jun, look at me. You will find yourself. You will see me again." She says to me as if she could read my mind. I smile softly at her. I slowly pull out of her embrace, walking over to my bed to grab the one thing that I cared to bring with me just in case I didn't make it, and couldn't come back. It was a picture of all of us. My mother, my father, and I. This was taken a few years back before he left us... No explanation, no note, nothing. We just woke up one day, and he was gone. I sat on the edge of the bed staring at it, wishing he were here today to see me off. I just wish he just was here period...

You can say that was the day my trust in the compound wavered. It didn't make sense to me. That was not something my father would ever do. From that day on, my investigation into his disappearance began. From how open and closed his case was, it just deepened the distrust I had for the compound.

"I miss him too Jun." My mother whispered with a longing in her voice. I jumped a little too, as I was lost in my own thoughts. I forgot that she was there.

I know I have to go today. The longer I sit here talking and thinking about it, the angrier I become. "Mom, this is so stupid. You can't even visit me! I'll be all alone, and so will you..." I choke out. I couldn't help it. There has to be more to this world than the shit-hole that I am living in now. There just has to be.

"Six months will be over before you know it Jun. As frightening as this is, you are going to learn so much. You are going to experience so much during your time there." She says. I can tell she is fighting the tears that are to fall. She is trying so hard to be strong for me. "As frightening as this is and will be, I met you father at Discovery and some of my dearest friends there. Our group was lucky. We only lost two people at the end of our time there. Some lose many more than that." She says the last part nonchalantly, and I'm not even gonna lie, it made my blood boil.

I sat there for a moment, quite shocked at the way she said that. She said it so flippantly, like it was no big deal. "How can you be so carefree about it? I could be one of those kids never to be seen again! This is so stupid! I still cannot wrap my head around the fact that everyone in this compound is okay with all of this!!" I say it louder than I meant too. I can see her physically shrink back at my words.

"It's not that I am so "*carefree*" as you put it. It's because it has been going on for so long that there is nothing anyone can do about it right now. People tend to not think about it, so they feel it absolves them of their guilt. For every soul that is lost, I feel it in my bones." She confesses.

At her words, my anger deflates. I know she feels it. My anger shouldn't be directed to her. "Mom, I'm just scared and I do not want to leave you." I say to her, as I give her another hug. I knew she meant no harm in her words, but when it comes to the compound, I have a really hard time controlling my emotions.

"What I would give to have you born on July 1, and not on June 30 right about now... Literally just one more day and I could have kept you for six more months..." She sighs against my shoulder.

Oh yeah. That is another thing. The reason that they only give you six months to find your 'true calling" is because they split you up, so there aren't so many people crowded in the sole building they have put aside for us to train in. Those born between January 1 - June 30 go in the first group of trainees. Then those born between July 1-December 31, go in the second group of trainees.

In the distance we could hear the footsteps approaching, signaling our time was almost up. You would think that they would want to keep as many people together since so many lives were lost, or drastically changed after the war. The council would say that was the reason the war happened in the first place. There were too many people, too many choices, and not enough punishment. Things were so black and white these days, there was absolutely no room for gray.

There was a knock at the door, and for a second I saw the tears in my mother's eyes threatening to spill over. Just as fast as they were there, they were gone. She wiped her tears away, hugged me a little tighter, then got up to go and answer the door. I took one more look around my room, burning it to memory before I followed her to the door.

"Mrs. Mikah, it is time." Said the one to the left. They had to send the enforcers to pick up the children who came of age now because a few years back, a whole group of families refused to give up their children for good, and tried to start an uprising. They figured if buff strong men armed with guns came to your door, you'd be less likely to fight back.

They were right.

I walked over to my mom with the photo in hand, and gave her the biggest hug I had ever given her in my life.

"Be strong Juniper, and know that I am always with you. I will always love you." She said as a few tears snuck out.

"I will mom. I love you too. I'll see you in six months." I say to her as convincingly as I could, trying to convince myself of the same thing.

"Make sure you have everything that you want to take with you." Said the one to the right. I looked up at him and he looked like he had seen many fights. You could tell he was hardened. The both of them had to be at least six and half feet tall.

I look over at my mother one last time before we leave. "Thank you, I am ready." Both of the enforcers nod to me, acknowledging that I am ready to go.

"Good day to you Mrs. Mikah." Both of them say as we make

our way to the front door. We step out into the hall and begin our journey to wherever I was to be living for the next six months. As we were walking away, I saw my mother standing in the doorway to our apartment. Her tears were flowing freely now as they were taking me away. My heart clenches, as my own tears start to spill at the sight of my mother breaking.

I'll see you soon mom.

I hope...

Chapter Two

It was a long and quiet walk through the corridors. I can't tell you how many turns we've made, or how far we've descended into the earth. Eventually we reach the bunker which will house me and all the other seventeen-year-olds in the first group for the next six months. It was a large open space that went up three floors. All along the outside of this room were doors lining up on every floor.

"Your room is number seven. All of the dorms are on the top floor. The middle floor is for learning trades, or training for a particular job that will give back to the community. The bottom floor, which is the one we are on, is for leisure. Best of luck to you." The one to left said as they both turned around and left.

Those were the first words they uttered to me since leaving my apartment. It was a long, quiet, awkward walk. I don't even think they blinked.

This
place
is
huge.

The apartment my mother and I shared was so tiny. We each had our own room, but the apartment given to us based on her credits. It was so very small. This place could easily fit one hundred plus of our apartments in it. It was shaped like a cylinder. A cylinder that stretched up three stories.

I slowly made my way up to the third floor. It seemed as though I was the first one here. I took my time and began to explore the first floor. There were couches, computers, board games, a bar, a pool table, and a cafeteria of sorts.

A bar?

They didn't think we were too young to drink? I wonder if it's a test set up to tease you. If you go for a drink, do you get thrown into the radiation? This is just asking for trouble, and I think I will be staying away from this. I wonder if this is how they weed out the weak ones, how they weed out the bad 'seeds', if you will. Unless they felt as though it was their way of making up, or the fact that these six months very well could be your last. Even if that were the case, it wouldn't be the best idea. Maybe if banishment/death wasn't a real possibility, it wouldn't bother me as much.

The walls were a bright white. They were as smooth as stone. The stairs that lead to the second floor were just behind the pool tables. At least they gave us something to do while we were all stuck here. I wonder if it is to take your mind off of the fact that you might not even make it out of here.

That you might be killed…

Or mutated…

Left for dead…

I can feel my stomach turn as it nearly makes me sick… Giving everyone a false sense of security.

The second floor was just door after door, and classroom after classroom. It also has one giant library and a gym. Had I not of been terrified of failing, I would have appreciated that library and gym a little bit more. I had no idea what I wanted to do. I had no idea what I wanted to contribute myself to for the better of the community.

My mother was a teacher. That type of life was not for me. Bless her heart though. I could not handle that many children at once. You have to be a special kind of person to be able to do that. My father was the complete opposite. He was an enforcer. An enforcer is someone who keeps the 'peace', who is also responsible for protecting us, and if on the off chance we run into anyone else (survivors on the outside), who are not friendly.

I always saw myself as an enforcer. My father would come home every night and teach me what he knew. We would spend hours training together... After his disappearance though, I couldn't even bring myself to think about it without tearing up, let alone train. I always thought I'd be one. But now? Now, I am not so sure.

I make my way up to the third floor, my dorm. By the time I get to my dorm, other people are dropped off and left to themselves. My dorm is bigger than my bedroom, so that's a plus. But everything seems so...so...plain. Gray walls, white and black sheets, and blankets. I really hope that we can change these. It is not very motivating. If anything, it makes you more nervous and depressed.

I make my way to my nightstand to place the photograph of my family and I on it. Once I place the photo on my nightstand, I turn my head to the left and see a giant desk. Something catches my eye, so I walk over to the desk seeing a piece of paper on it. It was a note to me:

"*Miss Juniper Mikah,*

Welcome to Discovery. We, the council, hope that within these walls, you will come to find what you can do for the good of this community, and what is good for you as well. For the next six months, you will be given a safe haven here to figure out what you can contribute to this compound.

Take tonight to familiarize yourself with Discovery. Get a feel for what you really want to do. Tomorrow, I will take a quick tour of all the classes and trades that are offered here. I'll be wandering around tomorrow, keeping an eye on everyone. Good luck, and goodnight.

Sincerely,

Senior Council Member - Jaila Montrose"

Jaila... I remember that name from one of my classes. We had to memorize everyone on the council and what they were responsible for. To be in her position though, there is no way that you can have a heart. To be able to send the kids away who don't make "the cut," to lead them to their death... I scrunched my face up in disgust. How could someone willingly do that? I am not looking forward to meeting her. Not one bit.

I looked around my room and just realized that there is not a bathroom in here... I really did not want to share a bathroom with a bunch of strangers. I hate being stared at for any reason.

I heard some commotion in the hallway and assumed the other kids were coming up, settling in. I get up off of my bed and make my way to my door. I open it, peeking outside. Sure enough, more and more kids were piling in downstairs. I could see them walking down the halls finding their own rooms.

I take a deep breath to calm my nerves. This was the most people that I have ever seen of the same age group in one place, ever. There had to be at least a hundred seventeen-year olds down there. To be honest, I was scared. I didn't even know that there were that many teenagers in the compound. That's a little intimidating.

I make my way down to the first floor, taking a seat in one of the lounge chairs. I noticed all of the kids around me. Some look happy to be here, some look sad, and some look absolutely terrified. I had a combination of sad and terrified, written all over my face. I knew it.

As I am looking around, I notice a girl with brown hair coming my way. She takes the empty seat next to me with a giant smile plastered on her face, and says, "Hello! My name is Hazel. Hazel McKenna. What's your name?" She asks a bit too bubbly for me. How can someone be so happy to be ripped away from their family?! I felt angry. Angry that this didn't seem to affect her as it did me. I take in an irritated breath as I squint my eyes at her. She looks confused. "Did I say something to offend you?" she asks. Does she really have no clue?

"How could you?" I said it a little bit harsher than I intend to. Her head tilts to the side like the fabled pets humankind used to keep before the war. So we were taught. Who knows if anything aside of the war was even true that they told us? In any case, animals now are strictly for food. That's it.

"I don't understand?" She says confused.

I roll my eyes at her "Obviously."

Abruptly, she stands up looking insulted. "You know what? Fuck you. I was just trying to be nice and sociable. You know, trying to become friends? We're all going to be stuck here for the next six months. Excuse me if I want to get to know you better and make friends. You can go and be miserable all by yourself. I'll stay clear of you from now on." She all but spit out.

She stands up to leave, and I immediately feel a little guilty. "Hey." I say to get her attention. "I just don't understand how you can be so happy is all." She gives me a dubious look.

"I'm sorry?" She asks, annoyed.

I inhale deeply, sadly. "It tore me apart to be ripped away from my mother, knowing that I run the very real possibility that I may never see her again. It pisses me off that the council can decide that at seventeen, you're ready to be on your own.

They decide the rest of your future, and that's only *if* you can make it through Discovery. After all is said and done, you could still end up being thrown out into the radiation. I mean, how someone can do that to someone else, knowing what could happen to them, I will never understand. You'd think that humankind would have learned from the last war. It's like people get some sort of sick, twisted pleasure administering harm on another human being(s). It makes me sick. Then hearing you sounding so excited to be here to be ready to face death? It angered me." I confessed to her.

Hazel looked down at the ground, her checks hot. I can't tell if she is crying silently, or thoroughly embarrassed. She looks back up at me, neither sad nor embarrassed. She looks pissed. "I'm sorry that you got ripped away from your *loving* family. I'm also sorry I don't share your hatred for leaving home. Let's just say I did not have the upbringing you clearly had. I could not wait to get away, too young to do so or not." She said it hotly. I could feel the anger rolling off of her in waves at the mention of her home life. I instantly felt horrible for the way that I acted. Maybe I shouldn't be so quick to judge...

I was speechless.

I wondered what could have happened to this young woman to make her want to leave her safe haven, her home. Especially because there was no guarantee that she would be able to stay. What could have happened to her that she had no fear of the radiation, mutation, or death?

"I am sorry. I guess I assumed that everyone felt the way that I did about being forced to leave your home with a very real possibility that we could be thrown out into the radiation. We could be left for dead." I explain this, feeling even more like a piece of shit as the time goes by.

She looked at me, and I was taken back a little. There was real fear and a burning rage simmering beneath the surface of that gaze.

"Well maybe you shouldn't just assume." She said pushing my shoulder back as she walked passed me. I deserved it. Again, I found myself wondering. What could have possibly happened to her to make her *want* to leave?

I was still in shock when another girl flopped down next to me. She wasn't as bubbly as Hazel, but still too bubbly for me. A blur of burgundy hair flew passed me as she sat, and a pair of striking hazel eyes stared back at me. With a grin almost the size of Hazel's, she stretched her arm out to shake my hand. "Hey, I'm Emelia Wright."

I took her hand in mine and shook it while I said, "I'm Ju-. My name is Juni." I decided to go by the nickname my parents always called me. It was a way for me to have a part of them with me always. Emelia was looking at me strangely.

"JuJuni? Well, that's ...*nice*." She said, trying to hide the fact that she thought my name was weird. I giggled a little bit, which in turn caused Emelia to giggle. "What is so funny?" She asks, in the midst of a giggle.

"That you thought my name is JuJuni. It's really Juniper. My parents always called me Juni and well, I figured having others call me that will keep them near me. Now that I say it out loud, it seems kind of silly." I say as I look at my hands, feeling silly.

"Hey, look up here." Emelia says as she points her fingers to her face. "I think it's beautiful. I'm sure your parents love that you'd want to keep their memory alive in you this way." She says still smiling. "So, what part of the compound are you from?"

"I'm from the northeast part of the compound. You?"

"I'm not too far from here actually. I used to pass here on my way to school." She said thoughtfully. "Are you scared Junip-, I'm sorry, Juni?" She said through a smile.

"I'm terrified. I'm angry. You name it." I told her. It was the truth.

She looked a little confused.

"I can understand being terrified. We all are whether some of us are willing to admit it or not. But why are you angry?"

I inhale sharply before I begin. As I exhale, I tell her how I felt about this whole situation. I can tell by her reactions to what I am telling her, that maybe she feels the same way.

16

"Wow, Jun. I can see why you are upset. But I don't think you are seeing the bigger picture..." My eyes must have looked like they were going to fall out of my head, because she quickly said, "What I mean is, although there is only a fraction of people left on Earth, I think they do this because they are afraid. They are afraid of what will happen if everyone succeeds." I could feel the rage bubbling up inside of me, the heat rising to my face.

"Excuse me?" I asked.

Emelia shook her head as she spoke. "Just think about it for a minute, will you? Relax before you get so defensive about it. Ther-."

My eyebrows furrow together, as my lips form a tight line. "You have got to be kidding me!" I scream. "You're going to sit here and tell me that you think it is okay to shove us into uncertainty? Not even good uncertainty? That they very well could be sending us to our deaths! And all of this because we may not be able to perform tasks which this council finds useful!" I was standing at this point, getting ready to walk off to my room.

Emelia's face was turning all different shades of red. "I never said that it was okay. I just said I could understand it." She said in a low, stern voice. It was almost menacing, and a little frightening. "Think about it, the human race has been living underground for nearly three hundred years. Sure, we have built up a small little underground city equipped to sustain what we have. But think about it, if we let everyone stay who can't serve to better the compound, they would be wasting resources that can't be replaced. It is a necessary cruelty." She says not showing a single shred of emotion behind that statement.

I can feel the scowl on my face grow the more she speaks. Is she serious? She actually agrees? I better work on my intuition. "Tsk, I guess you'll fit right in then. No worries for you Emelia, I just hope you feel this way when it is your child."

"That's not f- "

"What? You were going to say that it's not fair?! Well you know what's also not fair? Tossing the "unwanted" or "undesirables" out to die. Like there are just so many of us humans we could be tossed out like trash?!"

"Jun-"

"Do me a favor. Do me a favor and just don't. You know what the really sad part about all of this is? In three hundred years, the council hasn't even tried to come up with a better solution. They are perfectly okay with sending teenagers to their deaths." I spat.

It took all of my courage not punch her in the face for her ignorance. Am I the only one who feels this way? I really hope not, otherwise the human race is completely lost and we are no better off than we were three hundred years ago. "Just do me a favor Emelia, steer clear of me." I all but yell as I walk off. The fucking nerve of her. I bet at least one of her parents is on the council, or work with the council to have that kind of view on it.

I was on my way to my room when I passed a room with the door open. It was Hazel. She was in room five. I stopped and knocked on her door. I wanted to apologize for how I acted earlier. I also wanted to make some friends because as she so graciously pointed out, we are all stuck here for six months,whether we want to be here or not.

"Yes, who is it?" She asks.

"It's me, Jun." I say cautiously.

"You can keep walking." She says angrily.

"Please listen to me Emelia, hear me out. I just wanted to apologize for how I acted earlier, and for assuming. As you said, we are all stuck here for six months and we might as well be friendly to one another." I say hopeful. I hear her sigh, then some shuffling like she is getting up. She pushes the door open the rest of the way for me to come in.

"You're right. Because you were kind enough to apologize, I will be kind enough to accept your apology. Would you like to come in?" She asks.

I smile back at her. "Of course."

She steps aside so I can come in. Her room was the same as mine, right down to the placement of the furniture. From what I can see, she had brought nothing with her from her home. Much like me, except for my family picture. "So Hazel, what part of the compound do you come from?" I asked her that since I didn't get the chance to ask her earlier. Her jaw becomes taught, and that same look I saw in her eyes earlier comes back with a vengeance.

"If it is all the same to you, I'd rather not talk about my home life in any way, shape, or form. It's just too painful right now." She says looking down at her fidgeting hands. My heart breaks a little just at the thought of what she could have endured. It had to have been bad with the way she was acting.

I did as she asked, and I didn't ask again. I figured when she was ready, she would tell me.

We spent the rest of the night just shootin' the breeze. I told her about my family. I told her where we were from and how my dad just disappeared. She sat and listened, never veering into her own past. Even so, I couldn't shake the feeling that we are going to become great friends. A large smile spreads across my face, almost matching the one Hazel had when we first met. Suddenly Hazel gasps. "What?" I ask.

Giggling she says, "You do know what that is!"

I smile back, punching her in the arm. "Fuck you." I said through giggles.

Chapter Three

"What the fuck...?" My voice was thick with sleep. I woke up to a loud, obnoxious alarm. My hair was stuck to my face from drool and sweat. "Real nice Juniper." I say to myself as I wipe away the drool, fixing my hair. A loud screeching sound comes over the speakers in the ceiling (which I just noticed were there), and causes me to cover my ears. It was so loud that I swear I could feel it in my teeth.

"Attention! Good morning all new arrivals. My name is Jaila Montrose, and I will be watching over you for the next few months. I know you all must have some questions, and they will be answered in time. For today however, you need to focus on what it is you might be interested in pursuing while you stay here.

You can change your mind only once if you do not like your initial choice within the first three weeks. After three weeks, you will not be able to switch. This is because you will need the remainder of the time to train, and/or study in preparation for your chosen line of work. We give you this small gesture of kindness, because we understand what you are facing here. That is also why there is downtime space on the first floor. Drink responsibly, or you will no longer be permitted to do so. Any student can be expelled depending on the severity of what transpired.

You will hear this alarm four times a day. Once in the morning, once to indicate lunch, once to indicate the end of lunch, and once to signal the end of the day. After the last alarm is heard, that is your signal that class is over. You can begin your leisure activities. The morning alarm signals that you have forty-five minutes to get to class. Today however, the alarms are going to be different. Because today, you will tour what we have to offer you. You will hear an alarm every fifteen minutes, signaling that it is time to move on to another room. You will be free to choose what order in which to tour the classes.

"There is a button next to your night stand on the wall. Please push it to acknowledge that you heard and understood this message. I will be wandering around today watching over you. As of today, you are no longer children. You are considered adults. Welcome to Discovery! Have a good day, and good luck!"

I wipe my eyes some more in an attempt to rub away the sleepiness. I find the button on the wall and push it. I was not looking forward to hearing that godforsaken alarm all day today.

Okay, so forty-five minutes. I walk around to my closet, and see that there are clothes already in there for me to wear. Five pairs to be exact. One for casual occasions, one for formal occasions, a single dress, a pair of p.js. (in that moment I wish that I had looked in the closet last night because I slept in the clothes I wore yesterday), and a pair of work clothes. I looked down, and there were three pairs of shoes. All of them my size. A pair of sneakers, pair of heels, and a pair of work boots. I grab the casual outfit, a snug t-shirt, a pair of jeans, along with some clean undergarments, and sneakers. It was almost creepy that they knew my sizes, and that this was waiting for me. In the same regard, they knew who was coming before they did. There were not that many sizes to track down, so I guess that it is not too far-fetched to believe.

I shake that thought out of my head, grab my clothes, making my way to the door to go take a shower. Once I opened my door, I realized that I didn't know where the bathroom was. I did see the all the girls turning to the right once they walked out. Hopefully they were going to the bathroom too.

I felt a tap on my shoulder, so I turned around to see Hazel waving back at me. She is too awake right now.

"Hey friend! Good morning!" She says a bit too chipper. I look at her, and she laughs hysterically. "You're not a morning person are you?" She says through giggles. I roll my eyes, and grunt back at her. That causes her to laugh a little louder.

"You are way too happy, and awake way too early." I say to her sleepily. She just smiles at me as she pats my back.

"I have a feeling that we are going to be great friends." She says, reaffirming what I thought just last night.

We walked in silence the rest of the way to the end of the hall to the girl's bathroom. Once we got in there though, my heart sank a little. There were only six shower stalls with shower curtains. The rest had no curtains... This was not going to end well. That's for sure. All of the girls had the same look on their face. There were about twenty girls all staring at the stalls, then at each other. I looked at Hazel, and she looked terrified. I lowered my face to her ear and whispered, "I'm going for one, stay here. We will share. Hold my things, please." She looked up, and shook her head. I looked at the girl next to me, and she had the same expression on her face as I did. She was sizing me up. I smirked as I took off, a little amused at her. I took off first, but she was right on my heels. I leapt into the shower, and she followed suit. We stared each other down while circling the width of the shower. She had this look in her eye like she was starving, and I was a piece of meat.

She threw the first punch, which I dodged. We circled each other again. She throws a few more punches. One gets me right in the jaw, knocking me to the ground. Fuck. That is going to leave a mark. I stand up just as quickly as I go down. I know if I don't, I will be in for some nasty kicks. I rub my jaw on the way up. She smiles at me, obviously proud of herself. I'll let her savor the feeling a little bit before I counter back. She goes in again, this time more sure of herself. She throws a punch with a little more force this time, and I dodge it. This time though, as I dodge it, I use my right hand and uppercut her right in her ribs. She steps back gasping for air, looking at me in disbelief. I don't give her anytime to recover, quickly jabbing her in the throat as I sweep my right leg under her left leg. That sent her to the floor holding her throat, gasping for air. I can faintly hear Hazel cheering me on in the distance. I stand over her and kick her hand out of the way, and replacing it with my foot over her neck. She looks *pissed*. Good.

"Now you can try to keep fighting me, or you can give up and be my friend. I will share this shower with you. You decide. But let me just warn you, my father was an enforcer and taught me everything he knew in terms of self-defense. So I would seriously consider giving up. You cannot beat me." I say through confident, heavy breaths.

She just stares at me for a few minutes, trying to catch her breath. "Do you give up?" I ask again, a little impatiently. Her jaw is taught as she shakes her head yes. I immediately remove my foot from her throat, holding my hand out for her to take. Hesitantly, she takes it.

"My friend and I are going to take our showers first, then we will stand outside to make sure no one tries to hassle you while you take yours." I say to her. She just shakes her head yes in response. "Can I at least know your name?" I ask her trying to be nice, even though I just kicked the crap out of her. She is being a sore loser about it. I didn't have to share the shower with her after she tried to fight me for it. But as my father would say, "You'll catch more bees with honey than with vinegar."

"My name is Annia. Annia Nikols." Annia said with a scowl.

"Oh my god Jun! Where the hell did you learn how to fight like that? It was awesome!" Hazel screams as she comes running over.

I smile at her as I proudly say, "My father."

"Lucky you. You have to go and train to become an enforcer now that I have seen you in action!"

I shake my head no. "With as much fun as it would be, I

couldn't do it. Not with my father...." I say as I trail off.

Hazel realizing what she just said, covers her mouth in shock. "I am so sorry Jun. I, I wasn't thinking..." She says, her voice full of pity. And that right there, that was why I was always hesitant to tell anyone of my past history. This is the very reason. I didn't need, nor do I want anyone's pity. I swallow my pride and just let it go.

"Alright Hazel, Annia, since I did all the work in securing this shower, I am calling dibs on the first one." I said. Both of them roll their eyes, but make no objections.

I closed the shower curtain and get undressed. I yell to Hazel, "Catch!" as I toss my clothes over the top of the shower curtain.

"What the-oph! A little warning next time huh?! That would be nice." Hazel says.

I just laugh and say, "That my dear friend, is why I yelled catch." I can feel her roll her eyes and chuckle at the thought.

I turn the water on, adjusting it to the perfect temperature. I closed my eyes and just let the water hit me for the first ten minutes. It felt so good as the beads of water rolled down my body. It was so relaxing. I opened my eyes suddenly because I just remembered that I didn't have any shampoo or soap! "F u c k." I say to myself exasperatedly.

"What is it Jun?" Hazel asks, curiously.

I sighed loudly as I spoke, "I definitely forgot to bring shampoo and conditioner." I could hear the both of them laughing. "Yeah, yeah, hilarious. Can one of you go back to my room and see if you can find some in one of the drawers?"

"That's not why we are laughing." Annia says through her own giggle fit. "Look to the left side of the wall." Annia says.

"Okay, I am looking. What am I supposed to be seeing?" I asked.

"You really can't see it?" Annia asks, a little more in shock than anything else now.

"No. If I could I wouldn't be asking you for help now, would I?" I said it a little bit nastier than I meant to.

"You are going to feel like such an asshole once you see them. Open your fucking eyes." Annia says, as she laughs.

I don't know what she is trying to get me to se-.

Fuck.

I see it now, and I do feel like an ass. I hang my head and giggle. "You're right Annia, I do feel like an ass." I hear both of them giggle once more. I look to left side of the shower and sure enough, there are three pumps; shampoo, conditioner, and body wash. I finish and get out, letting the other two take their turns. They were faster than I was, which was good. I didn't want to stand there for too long, and it gave us time to brush our teeth.

"So Annia, now that we're not trying to kill each other over a shower, do you want to tour the classes with Hazel and I today?" I ask her. Hazel gives me a questionable look. Annia looks at me the same way as Hazel does. I roll my eyes. "You don't have to if you don't want to. I can let the shower incident go if you can. As my friend Hazel pointed out to me yesterday, we're stuck here for six months. We might as well be friendly."

"She's right Annia, come with us." Hazel says.

Annia finally agrees with a smile playing at her lips. "Alright."

I smile, "Good. Where do you want to go first?" Annia looks at me almost like she is embarrassed. I roll my eyes, "Where?"

She sucks her upper lip into her mouth averting her eyes from me, to the floor, then the ceiling. Was she embarrassed? Finally, she clears her throat before she says, "I want to learn how to be a caretaker." She says it so low that I almost don't hear her. I look at her quite puzzled. Why on earth did she feel embarrassed by that? Then I hear Hazel stifle a laugh. Annia didn't seem to hear her though. Thank god. I shoot Hazel a death glare, which causes her smile to fade almost instantly.

"Why is it a secret that you want to do this?" I ask Annia, truly curious.

She looks at me for a few minutes before she speaks. "Because when I admit that to someone, they usually laugh at me." I look at her even more perplexed.

"What the heck is so funny about it?" I asked, now completely confused.

"Not many people want to get into this part of the healthcare field. Most people want to be doctors, or even nurses. No one really ever goes for being a caretaker, because they do not want to babysit babies or care for the elderly. But what they don't realize is that somebody has to do it, and with so few people left on this planet, we can't just brush them off. It is a job that has to be done. But for me, it is more than that. I *want* this line of work. I say this because I watched my grandmother go through hell, and I couldn't do anything about it. It gives me peace of mind actually. It gives me peace of mind to know that all the elderly and children I take care of will be treated like my very own family." She says.

I think about it for a minute. Then it dawns on me why everyone she told laughed at her. She does not look like the type of person that would *want* to help take care of babies and the elderly. She is a full foot shorter than I am at five feet eight, she has short black hair, with an athletic build. She also gives off this vibe that screams *'stay the hell away from me!'*.

"Okay, we're off to the caretaking class first." I notice Hazel roll her eyes.

"What?" I ask.

With a loud huff she says, "I really was hoping to skip that particular class. It holds no interest for me whatsoever."

"Come on Hazel, I am sure that there will be classes that she goes to with us that she really does not want to go to. But if you really feel that strongly about it, we can always just meet up later." I say it a little annoyed that she can't put up with fifteen minutes of the class. She looks at me as if she is really thinking about it. "You seriously can't sit through fifteen minutes?" I ask, utterly shocked.

She rolls her eyes and just as she is about to speak, Annia cuts her off. "It's no big deal really. I'll just go by myself. I'll probably be in there all day anyway."

I give Hazel a dirty look. "Annia, I'll go with you." She just shakes her head no.

"I don't want to be a bother. Your plans didn't involve me to begin with. Maybe we can meet up for lunch or something?"

"I'd love to." I say to Annia. She smiles a smile that doesn't reach her eyes. It's almost like a sad smile. As she walks away, I turn and look at Hazel with the dirtiest, most pissed off look I can muster.

"What?" She asks a bit testy.

I narrow my eyes at her as I feel the anger rolling off of me. "What the hell was that about? Do you have something against her? You did invite her as I did to come with us. Did you really think that we would skip that class?"

"I do not have anything against her. I just really did not want to go to that class." She stats matter-of-factly.

"So your solution to this was to make someone we invited to come along with us feel like crap? Did you even think of how that would make her feel?" I say as the irritation builds.

Hazel sighs loudly, "No... I guess I didn't. When you think about it, I did come off as a giant bitch huh?" I raise my eyebrows, and shake my head once.

"I think you owe her an apology at lunch." I say.

"Yeah, I think you're right." She sighs.

"Alright, alright. Enough of that stuff. What class should we attend first?" Hazel taps her mouth thinking about what she would want to look into first.

"Hmmmm." She says, "I think I would like to look at some of the intelligence classes first." I look at her in amazement for a few seconds. I swear it was like she was reading my mind. I had my own motives for my interest in wanting to learn the intelligence field. I was hoping that it might give me some leads on my father's disappearance. I wasn't going to trust anyone with that information. I had decided that was my plan last night. It was a good decision for the compound, and a good decision for me.

"That sounds great. I am not sure yet what I want to do, but I know I definitely wanted to look into some of those classes." I say smiling. She smiles back as we make our way to the second floor, with Hazel being unaware of my true purpose. To our surprise, there was only one class for each type of job. I wondered why that is?

We make our way to the intelligence class, finding a seat next to each other in the middle of the room. Our teacher was sitting at her desk looking over papers. To my surprise, she didn't look too much older than I was. For a brief moment, I let my mind wander and wonder what you would have to do to teach, or if it was a punishment of some sort.

After a few minutes, the room fills up and our instructor gets up to close the door. She was very pretty. She was maybe five foot five, but her pumps made her at least five foot seven. She had an athletic build that you could see through her dress, and long strawberry blonde hair that waved out towards the ends. She also had a strong, powerful walk that demanded attention. I noticed it as she walked past me.

"Hello, my name is Melanie and I will be your instructor for at least the next three weeks. If you hang around, you'll have me for the next six months. You are all probably wondering why there is only one class for this field, when there are so many fields within this field alone. Well to answer this question, if you graduate from Discovery you will be placed in the lowest position this field has to offer. How you learn and how you use that knowledge to contribute to your field will determine how quickly you move up the ranks. As you move up, you will be trained by someone in the field that you were promoted to. Please keep in mind that you may never be promoted, especially in the intelligence field. It is not your right to be promoted just because you have been in the same position for five years, and if people that have just got in are promoted before you, tough cookies. You earn your place here, nothing is handed out.

"Lying, treachery, cheating, stealing, bullying, and secrets, are not kept or tolerated among those in intelligence. In order for this operation to run smoothly, we all need to trust one another. If you are caught doing anything that even remotely resembles any of the aforementioned, you will be tossed out to take your chances with the radiation. If by some miracle you survive, you will be banned from the compound."

"That being said, there are different levels of clearance that are given based on your field level. The higher levels of the security clearances do not need to share sensitive information with lower level clearances. The lower level clearances have to however, share everything."

"Period."

"There are absolutely no exceptions to this rule. If we let you slide, then we have to let everyone slide. If you are lucky enough to be a part of the chosen few who pass this class and move on into the intelligence career field, you will be privy to highly sensitive information. We need to know you can be trusted. If it gets out that you have been selling information for credits, or giving information away, you will be thrown out immediately."

"That being said, if you are looking for the thrill of your life, to be challenged at every turn both physically and mentally, to be kept on your toes, and live one hell of a fulfilling and exciting life, intelligence is for you. I've been in the intelligence field for the better part of five years now, and I've never looked back." She says as she walks the classroom. "Are there any questions?" She asks as her eyes scan the room. A tall, built boy raised his hand. "Yes, you in the back. Please state your name before your question."

He smirks as he says, "My name is Decland Riehner, and I was curious as to what we can expect to learn in this class, and why it is that you are teaching it?"

Melanie's right eyebrow raised a little taken, I guess by Decland's comment. She looks at him steeling her facial expression, standing tall. "Can I ask why it is that you question my ability to teach this class?" She asks in an authoritative tone. He looks at her, not even trying to hide the smirk on his face. He was definitely taller than her, and he definitely has more muscle than her.

"You honestly think that you could take me in a fight? You're far too pretty to be getting into fights with men, or have anything worthwhile up here." He says as he points to his head. What an asshat! I hope she knocks him out.

She smiles humorously at him. "Well I would hope my superiors knew what they were doing when they promoted me to the stealth team. You have to be promoted at least six times before you're even considered for that promotion. But if you feel you are smarter than they are, why don't you try and put me in my place." She says to him, now mere inches from his face.

An evil glare reaches Decland's eyes at her statement. His facial expression alone says that he can take her. The boy oozes confidence. I'll give him that. His statement about women not having much 'up there' though makes me want to get up and kick his little boy parts.

Asshole.

"Aren't you afraid you'll break a nail or those pretty shoes?" He asks, taunting her. She just smiles back at him as she goes to look at her shoes. As she does that, the sneaky fuck suddenly makes his move to try and take her down when she isn't looking at him.

What a coward!

He closes his hands together, and tries to smash them into her back. As he is bringing his hands down, I am almost positive that I see her smile. When she grabs her right heel I know that I was right; she turns it up so the heel is facing out towards Decland. She thrusts it up and hits him right in between the legs. Instantly his face becomes pale as he drops to the floor, huffing as all the air comes out of his body at once. As he is rolling around on the floor in agony, I smile. As I'm smiling, Melanie looks at me smugly. Good for her, and good for that asshat. He got what he deserved.

"Anyone else feel the need to question my ability to teach this class?" She asks, daring anyone else to challenge her. Everyone is silent and I am assuming still in shock, because no one makes a sound. That's probably a good idea on their part.

"I'll take the silence as a no. As per the first part of Mr. Reihner's question, I cannot get into the specifics of what you will learn in this class until after your first three weeks. That is when you will no longer be able to switch classes. As to why I am teaching this class, once you graduate from Discovery you will at some point have to teach a class. Every few rotations someone is picked to teach. You might even have to do it more than once in your lifetime. You may also get lucky and never have to. This time it was my turn to teach. One piece of advice I will share with you, is to never judge someone based on their looks. Looks can be deceiving. That is the reason I dressed like I did today." She says, as she walks the classroom looking at everyone. One would almost say she was sizing up everyone. "Are there any more questions? Our time here today is almost up."

You know, come to think of it, my mother nor my father had to teach, at least not in my lifetime. Melanie seems so confident, and why not? She just took down the biggest seventeen-year old I have ever seen. She is smaller than I am, and she did this in heels...and a dress... I raise my hand suddenly, very interested in this career. "You in the middle, state your name before your question."

"Hello. My name is Juniper Mikah." At the sound of my name, her mouth drops for a second as recognition washes over her face. It happened so fast that I am not sure if it really did. "I was wondering what you *could* tell us?"

Just as she was about to answer the question, that hideously loud annoying alarm sounds. She smirks as she says, "Come back tomorrow Miss Mikah, and I will tell you."

"Just my luck." I say to Hazel as we gather our things to go to the next class. We pass Decland and some of his friends are trying to help him up but he keeps swatting them away, yelling at them. I assume he is trying to save face.

What a loser.

"Can you believe what just happened!?" Hazel laughs as we get into the hallway.

I smile back at her, just as amused. "He deserved it. So what do you think so far? Is intelligence something that you think you're still into?" I ask Hazel.

"I don't know. I would like to learn more about it before I completely commit to it, you know? I'd hate to choose it then after the three weeks go by, be stuck in it because she teaches stuff I do not like or agree with." She says.

She has a point. "I like what I've seen so far from the class. I'll go through the other classes just to be sure though."

"You're really that sure?" She asks, curiously.

I smile at her as I say, "Well, I can't bring myself to be an enforcer. If I am in intelligence, I can still help people that way, and you know, still protect them." *And hopefully find out what happened to my dad*, I say to myself.

"Ahhh, okay. I can see it now." She says to me.

We go from class to class with nothing really catching my eye. My mind is still on the intelligence class. Once the bell rings, we head for the first floor to meet up with Annia for lunch.

"So what did you think of that last class!?" Hazel asks, her eyes are dancing with amusement.

I roll my eyes. "Ugh, that was so disgusting! I give a lot of credit to the compound public area cleaners. I could never do that! You think that being stuck underground, people would want to be cleaner... Ewe..." I say the last part as a shiver runs down my spine. I have a new found respect for them now, that is for sure. Hazel just laughs at me.

Just as Hazel and I get in line to grab our food, we see Annia walk in. We wave her over and let her cut in front of us amongst the protest of the others, especially Decland.

"Hey! No cutting!" He yells from the back of the line.

"Oh can it Decland! Unless you plan on underestimating me too? Better yet, come and try me. Let me embarrass you more, shall I?" I yell back at him standing defensively. "There'll be plenty of food left for you. One person will not add any more time to your wait."

"This is bullshit." He mutters under his breath, but quiets up.

"What's his problem?" Annia asks as she steps in front of me.

"He's just pissed because his ass got handed to him by the intelligence instructor who's half the size of me, and was in a dress and heels." I giggle. Annia laughs as she rolls her eyes. "How was your caretaker class?"

Her eyes light up as she says, "It was amazing! I didn't even bother going to the other classes! I know that is where I am supposed to be!" She says confidently. "How was yours?"

"I feel the same way about the intelligence class. I checked out a few more other classes, but they didn't interest me in the slightest."

"Yeah, she didn't even pay attention in the other classes. As for me, I just don't know yet. There are so many options." Hazel says.

"You know you could try out the class Annia is in." I say casually.

"I suppose." Hazel says.

"You never know Hazel, you might just find your calling." Annia says. "Plus there are so many different opportunities in that field. It's not just about caring for the elderly or babies."

"You could be right." Hazel says.

We grab our food and find a table. We fill the time with idle chit chat and by the end of lunch, Hazel still has no idea what she wants to do. She agrees to go into the caretaker class after lunch just to see what it is about, since she is still undecided. We each part ways to our rooms after lunch, totally exhausted. We try and take a quick cat nap before rotations begin again.

I had no luck falling asleep. All I could think about was Melanie, and the face she made when she heard my name. Did she know my father? I am interrupted from my thoughts by that damned bell,while making my way to the next class. I don't even remember what it was or the classes that followed, because my mind was still back in the intelligence class.

The last bell rang signaling the end of the day. I make my way back to the leisure room to find Hazel and Annia. They were nowhere to be found.

Huh… I wonder where they could be? I grab something quick to eat, deciding to make it an early night. I wanted to be prepared and well rested for what was to come tomorrow.

I walk into my room and decide to take a shower tonight so I am not fighting for one in the morning. I'm not going to lie, walking down these hallways at night is a little creepy. You can hear every noise in the dimly lit hallway because it was so quiet. Once I make it to the showers, I am happy to see that no one else had the same idea. I place my things, take off my clothes, and jump in.

Once I am in the shower again, I let the water hit me. As the time passes, my mind wanders back to the intelligence class. It wandered back to that look that Melanie gave me again when I told her my name. I am almost positive now that she reacted to it. Did she know my father? I am going to have to ask her about that tomorrow.

Chapter Four

"Alright class, let's begin." Melanie says as the last few students pile in and take their seats. Today there were more boys than girls in this class (one other than me). I half expected that. The girls who were in here yesterday did not seem to be too interested in the class.

Melanie was scanning the room like she was looking for someone, or something. Once her eyes fall upon me, she stops.

"To answer a question that was asked yesterday, but was never answered; during the first three weeks you will be learning self-defense. That is the only thing that you can learn that protects our secrets, and will benefit you in the long run. That being said, the first three weeks you will be training with the enforcers. Both careers learn the same basics when it comes to defense. Only later on in the careers do they begin to differ. Are there any questions before we head out to join the enforcers in the training room?" Melanie asks.

I have to admit, I am a little shocked. I didn't think the intelligence career path included stuff like this. Melanie saw my face and smirked. I know my face betrayed me, showing just how confused I actually was.

"Awe Juniper, you didn't think we were all nerds who couldn't protect ourselves did you?" She taunts.

I smile back. "I am just a bit shocked is all. I really shouldn't be seeing what I saw yesterday. Hearing that we are undergoing training to defend ourselves is a bit overwhelming and exciting at the same time." She just smiles back as she makes her way to the door.

"After what you saw yesterday? Did you think I was born able to fight? You must know how to act in all situations. Whether it be defending yourself against an enemy, gathering intelligence, or playing a role. You must be on your toes at all times, always be ready to improvise at a moments notice." She says this as we walk down the hall to the training room. She stops in front of a pair of large double doors before she opens them. "I want you all to know that this gym never closes. You are free to train here at any time, for as long as you need." She says reassuringly.

She opens the doors and a giant room stands before me. Anything, and everything you could imagine is in this room. Punching bags, salmon ladders, weight benches, sparing rings, etc... I was in awe.

I could hear the enforcer instructor just ahead, instructing his students. "You must always have your guard up! Be prepared for anything, at any time. In this line of work, you will find yourself in many situations that are less desirable than others; certain things that you may not agree with. But it is our job to enforce the laws set forth by our council. We must uphold the law, enforce the law, and protect the innocent civilians of this compound. The human race suffered a great blow due to their own hands. We may never be able to repopulate the surface of the earth again. We may never again reach the greatness that it once was. That is why it is of the up most importance to protect the population now. Every human life is precious." He says with his voiced raised slightly, demanding their attention as he speaks.

I almost laugh at the end of his speech though. 'Every human life is precious...' Is that some sort of sick joke? If 'every human life' was so precious, then why would we throw our own children into the radiation just because they had nothing to offer the compound? Why just toss people out there for breaking the laws or failing here?! Hell, they probably do it for looking at you the wrong way. I wonder if they really believe that, or if that is something that they all tell each other to cope with what they have to/choose to do sometimes.

The enforcer instructor turns his head our way, smiling brightly. He looks so young to be an instructor. He can't be any more than twenty years old. He has to be at least six feet tall. He has a muscular athletic build, with black hair cut short to the scalp. Not buzzed, but short. Then I see his eyes... They are a piercing baby blue, with tattoos going up both of his arms.

"Ahh Melanie! What a pleasant surprise. I didn't know that you would be teaching this time around." He says to our instructor, breaking me from my daze.

Daze?

No, not possible. I can't be attracted to anyone right now, let alone an instructor. He broke my *assessment* of him; yeah assessment, not *daze.* Pull your head out of your ass Juniper.

She smiles back at him. They must be old friends.

"I am. It's nice to see a friendly face here to work with me for the next three weeks." She says. Then she gets this anticipated look on her face. "Are you ready to whip these "*adults*" into shape?" She asks as she smirks. He smirks back at her, moving to the side to give her the floor.

"Alright, listen up! For the first week, the men and the women will be training separately. During the second and third week, you will be fighting each other. The first week will not be graded, but the last two weeks will be graded. It will go towards your overall grade at the end of the six months." She shouts it so everyone could hear her. "For those of you who do not know me, I am Melanie, Instructor for the Intelligence class." The instructor for the enforcer class smiles at her.

"And for those of you who do not know me, my name is London. London Cheri." I hear a couple of giggles throughout the crowd. This just seems to make him smile more wickedly.

I could swear I see Melanie smile the same way, like she knows what he is doing. "Go on, get in a few good laughs. Everyone has a good laugh at my last name." He says as a few more laughs erupt around me. "Now that you got your good laugh in, if I hear it again, you will personally have to answer *to me*." He says as he slams his fist into his open palm. Suddenly, all of the laughing stops abruptly.

"All of the men are going to come with me, and all of the women are going to go with Melanie." London says. "Alright, let's get this show on the road." He says as he starts to walk towards the punching bags.

"Alright ladies, during the first week you will learn how to defend and protect yourself should you ever find yourself in a fight. The worst thing you could ever do is underestimate your opponent. As some of you witnessed yesterday, a young man underestimated me because I am short. I was in a dress, and was wearing high heels. He learned that day... Well I hope so at least, to not underestimate me again. Do any of you have any training in hand to hand combat?" I hesitate for a moment looking around to see if anyone does, or is brave enough to step forward. To my surprise, no one steps forward. Okay, I'll just bite the bullet.

"I am." I say as I step forward. She smirks at me, giving me a knowing look.

"Alright then. Let's see what you are made of. Put em' up!" She shouts.

We both raise our hands, standing in a defensive stance. We start to circle each other, sizing one another up. She goes in first attempting to jab my ribs, but I block her and push her off. She looks taken by surprise at first, then smiles. A determined look flashes across her face. We begin to circle each other again and this time, I make the first move. I drop to the ground sweeping my right leg into her calf so fast that she doesn't even see it coming, and falls to the ground. In an instant, we are back on our feet. She gets up and doesn't waste any time. She lunges forward jabbing me in the gut, throwing another jab into my face, finally stomping on my left foot. I stumble back out of breath with my chest heaving. Holy fuck! I better stop holding back or she is going to take me out. I see the grin on her face. She's satisfied. Well, I will now have to show her what my dad really taught me.

I shake my head and put my hands back up, completely ready to go. "Are you sure Juniper? We could always stop now." She says taunting me. What a bitch, but it's working.

"I was taught to never quit. I am not stopping unless you can knock me out." I spat. Her smile widens, amused and expecting.

"Bring it then. Let's give them a real demonstration, and stop holding back." How did she know I was holding back? Before I could think too long on that thought, she was coming at me throwing punch after punch. I was dodging them, desperately trying to find a place she wasn't guarding. The whole time I was picturing sparring with my dad. I could hear him in my head. *'Come on Juni, keep your hands up! You can do better. Try and STOP me.'* I raise both of my arms, trapping her arms under me at my sides, headbutting her twice, causing her to stumble backwards once I released her hands. I take this opportunity to make my move and finish this fight. I run, launching a flying roundhouse kick to the right side her face. She falls to the ground, instantly knocked out.

From the corner of my eye, I can see London running full speed in our direction. He kneels down next to Melanie, giving her a once over. She starts to move a little while he does this, and you can see him visibly relax a bit at her movement. "Jesus Melanie, you scared the shit out of me when I saw you drop like a stone." Melanie slowly sits up rubbing her jaw.

"Nice Juniper. Your father taught you well." At that statement, London and I looked at her confused. I knew she reacted the way that she did when I told her my last name! She knew him!

"I'm sorry, you knew my father? How? He was an enforcer, not Intelligence." I asked, truly wanting to know. As far as I knew, he wasn't friends with anyone outside of the enforcers.

London looked utterly confused at my admission.

"That Juniper, is a question for after class. Good job." She says while London helps her up. I can't believe she would say something like that, then refuse to tell me anything more. She could see the frustration written all over my face. She places her hand on my shoulder as she says, "I will tell you all about it after class today. Don't stress over it, okay?"

I sigh, "Okay."

"Wow, I don't believe it." London says, amazed.

"What?" Both Melanie and I ask.

"You got your ass handed to you! On the first day none the less! I'm going to have to keep my eye on you Juniper." He says. Melanie shoots him a death glare. I couldn't help it, as soon as he said that I could feel the heat rise to my cheeks. Oh man, I hope no one notices...

No such luck...

"Well well Juniper, is that blush I see?" He teases. At those words, I blush an even deeper shade of red. I hear him chuckle. "Good to know." *Good to know?* What does that mean? And why when he said that, did my heart begin to race?

Oh fuck, no, no, no. I won't let it happen.

"Alright alright. You can tease each other and stare into each other's eyes all you want after class. And you sir, better watch who you tease about being knocked out. Do you remember the last time we sparred. I do. Wasn't it *you* who got knocked out?" She teased him. London rolled his eyes.

"You got in one lucky shot. Will I never live that down?" He asks.

"Never. You got knocked out by a woman half your size." She laughed as he rolled his eyes again.

"Yeah. Okay, you got lucky. Alright, let's get back to our classes huh? I just wanted to make sure you were okay." He said as he started to jog back to his class. Just before he turned, I could have sworn I caught him checking me out. Once he reaches my eyes, he *winks*.

Shit.

He was checking me out. What's worse is he caught me...

I hang my head.

Dammit.

I look over at Melanie and she is smirking at me. "Alright class, were you watching the stances and forms of the both of us while Juniper and I were sparring?" She asks, taking her attention off of me...

Thank god.

I can't believe I let myself slip the way that I did. I look at the class, all ten of them. Their mouths are hanging open. Sure, London was very good looking, but I couldn't like anyone that way right now. I have to focus on graduating from Discovery. I couldn't risk being thrown out because of a stupid crush. That's it. It's settled. No matter what, my focus HAS to remain on graduating, definitely not boys. A particular one named London to be precise.

I was so lost in my thoughts that I completely tuned out Melanie. I kept glancing her way and saw that she was showing them certain techniques, having them try the techniques on each other.

"Alright class!" Melanie yells, "So far you have done very well. Some of you need more work than others. That is okay. Do you remember what I told you before we walked in? This gym never closes. Feel free to practice anytime that you need to. For the next thirty minutes, we are going to jog around the gym." Everyone moans loudly at that. "I know it sucks, but it's the best thing for you and it will help build up your stamina. Get moving!" She screams, leaving no room for protest.

Everyone began to jog. As we passed London's class, he stopped his class and sent them to jog with us. He then joined Melanie in the office attached to the gym.

"Hey Juniper!" I hear someone yell. I turn my head around to see a girl with black hair and metallic blue highlights waving her hands, running towards me. Who is-? Ohhh Emelia. When did she get highlights? And change her hair? I really did NOT want to talk to her...

"Hey Emelia. What's up?" I ask, not very enthused.

"Not much. So, the intel class huh?"

"Yeah. Are you in London's class?"

She smiles brightly as she shakes her head. "I saw you knock out Melanie! How crazy was that? How on earth did you learn to fight like that?" She asked.

"My father was an enforcer and insisted on teaching me everything he knew in self-defense. He said that he wasn't going to have me leaving the house alone unless I knew how to defend myself." I say this a little sad.

Emelia catches that and asks, "Are you okay?"

"Yeah. It's just... I haven't seen my father since I was fourteen. He just vanished into thin air. No note, nothing. He was just gone..." I say to her with a longing in my voice. I really missed him. I guess it is so hard because we never got closure. My mother and I, we never understood. My father wouldn't just leave his family. There were no reports of anyone being tossed out into the radiation. When they do that they announce it, whether it's a new trainee who has failed or someone being punished. They wanted to let *everyone* know. I guess it was their way of scaring people into being good, obedient citizens.

Disgusting.

Her face drops a little. "I am sorry Juni. I didn't know."

"It's okay." I say as I exhale.

"So is it me, or is London super-hot?!" She squeals. Again my body betrays me, and blush creeps into my cheeks. Emelia laughs at me. "I knew it! You think so too! I would take this class over and over if he taught it every time."

"You would choose a career or something that would shape the rest your life, even if you didn't like it at all, to look at a cute boy?" I ask, utterly confused. I would never do such a thing.

Did I just mention he was cute?

She looks at me now confused. "You wouldn't?" I laugh lightly as I shake my head no. She shrugs and we continue our quiet jog until she sees someone else, saying bye to me. Thank god. She seems nice enough. I just didn't want to be bothered.

Not to mention the last conversation we had...

The rest of my jog sucked. After ten minutes I felt like I was going to die. I swear I could feel someone watching me, but every time I turned around there was no one there. I thought I was beginning to lose my mind. The last few minutes of my jog I was almost walking because it hurt so bad.

"TIME!" Melanie yells, after blowing her whistle. I nearly fall to my knees. Here I am thinking I'm in good shape... What a freaking joke. "Alright, we're going to do some stretches then you are free to go to lunch." Melanie says.

We spend the next ten minutes doing all different kinds of stretches. Melanie dismisses the class mere seconds before the alarm goes off, but waves me over to her. "I know you must have a lot of questions. I will answer what I can, just let me know when you are ready." She says.

I stare at her for a moment, once again wondering how she knew my father. Were they friends? Did they work together? How would they even have worked together? Did she know him at the time he disappeared? I realize that I am staring.

"I'm sorry if I am staring, it's just a lot to take in. I have so many questions to ask you, but I get the feeling that asking them here is not a smart idea." I say as I look around.

She smirks at me. "I think you will do just fine in this class Juniper. You are very perceptive. There is a lot that you, well really everyone, doesn't know about. There is so much that I have to tell you. First things first, I will talk to you about your father. Meet me tonight in the girl's bathroom. It is the only place in Discovery that is not being watched or listened to. The only reason is because it is illegal."

I give her a questioning look as I ask, "What do you mean that is the only place not being watched or listened to?"

"Discovery has cameras all over it, except your rooms and the bathrooms. I thought it would less conspicuous if we walked into the girl's bathroom instead of either one of our rooms."

"Wait, the teachers stay in here too? Why is that? Don't some of you have a family?" I ask, utterly shocked at the thought that they would have to stay here away from their families for six months to 'train the newly appointed adults.'

"It is all part of fulfilling your duty to the compound. Besides, it's only six months. It's not like it's forever." She says, matter-of-factly. "The instructors are not allowed to leave, however your family can visit you on your down time, so it really isn't that bad."

I roll my eyes at that statement. Give me a freaking break. *'For the duty to the compound.'* Part of that is throwing people into the radiation for no other reason then they don't fit the mold that the council tries to create.

Sickening.

For a moment, I think I see Melanie smirk. But just as quick as it appeared, it was gone. "I'll see you at ten o'clock." She says as she walks past me out of the doors.

Even though my legs are on fire, I decided to stay and hit the punching bag for a bit. I walk across the gym to the bags and begin with jabs. I feel eyes on me. *Again.* This time I see London walking my way. For some reason my heart begins to beat faster at the site of him.

Dammit.

I continue to hit the bag, acting like he doesn't affect me. I will take my frustrations out on this bag. I will not let myself be *that* girl. Well, he isn't *technically* my instructor.

Stop that.

Focus on getting out of Discovery alive, not about his lips…

Fuck…

I just hang my head and attempt to shake that thought out of it. I keep my eyes focused on the punching bag as he approaches me.

"I was highly impressed when I saw you knock out Melanie. She also seems to know your father, whom you say was an enforcer. Care to share who he might be?" He asks as he stands behind the punching bag, facing me. There was a slight smirk on his face.

I finally look at him, incredulously.

"What? I know all of the enforcers past and present. I would like to know who your father is." He asks.

"I really don't know you, so I am not going to tell you who my father is. Just know that I'm able to defend myself if the need should arise." I say this as I punch the bag a few more times, making my point.

He smiles at me. "Oh I think I know that." He says as he chuckles. He licks his lips as his brows furrow, his eyes slit like he is thinking of something. I try not to stare at his lips, but I can't help it. At that moment he sees it.

Fuck.

His smile grows wider as he steps in front of the punching bag, forcing me to stop hitting it.

My breath stops in my throat and my head becomes mush. He is so *good looking*.

Snap out of it! I yell at myself.

"Well, maybe we can change that?" He asks as he leans in closer to me, placing his hands on my shoulders licking his lips, sucking on them a little bit. They burn at his touch. I wake up in that instant and back away from him. A confused look passes across his face. "I'm sorry, I guess I read that wrong. "He says stepping back looking a little embarrassed.

I blink my eyes a few times, shaking my head in an attempt to clear it. "No.. No, you didn't read that wrong. I find you incredibly attractive." He smiles widely at my admission, as my cheeks burn from it. "Right now though, I need to focus on getting out of Discovery alive." I say to him, once I find my voice.

I am looking everywhere but his face. I look at the floor, my shoes, and the salmon ladder behind him. Another thought crosses my mind, and my cheeks burn even brighter. I groan. He just chuckles like he knows why.

"I think you will be just fine here." He says as he tries again to come closer to me. I back away again, placing my hands on his chest to stop him.

Oh my. His chest is tight. I allow my hands to linger for a bit longer than they should have...

"You are also an instructor, and I am a trainee. Your trainee too. For the next three weeks anyway... Not to mention that you are older than me...." I say, finally looking at him. Once I do, all of the air leaves my body.

He lifts his hand and gently brushes my hair out of my face. He looks at me and I swear he can see straight through me, making my heart race. He raises his other hand places it over my heart, laughing as he licks his lips *again*. I know he can feel how fast it's beating. He takes his hand out of my hair to pick up my hand and place it over his heart. To my surprise, it is also racing. I look at him confused. Could he really find me attractive? He did just try to kiss me...

"You see, you have the same effect on me. As far as my age, I am only four years older than you. Is that really too much for you?" He says, just inches from my face while staring at my lips.

My breath stops in my throat, and the ability to think straight is gone. I stare at his lips and shake my head no, unable to speak. He places both his hands on either side of my face, rubbing his thumbs gently across my cheek bones. He looks into my eyes for a second before his searing gaze falls to my lips once again.

In that instant I swore my heart stopped. I forget how to breathe. My heart beats louder and faster the closer he gets. My hand is still on his chest, his heart beating faster the closer he gets to me. Just as he is about to place his lips on mine, the door to the gym opens and a few people walk in causing us to back away from each other.

The moment is gone, the spell is broken.

What the fuck was that?

Thank god to anyone that came in.

I look at him and can't believe how close I came to just throwing it all away. How could I be so *stupid*!

Stupid girl.

That is why I won't let myself become so distracted by a boy. I take one more glance at him before I leave. I hear him call my name, but I just keep walking. I couldn't let myself get so distracted again. It was like I was in a trance. I couldn't stop myself when I was that close to him.

I ran straight to my room to grab some clothes, then to the showers to clean not only the workout off of me, but to clear my head of London. I can't worry about anyone or have that type of relationship right now. I *can't* risk it.

As I get out of the shower I hear the bell signaling that lunch is over. I hope the next half of the class is in the classroom. After what happened, I couldn't even look at London right now.

I make my way to class, sitting in my seat as my other classmates get into theirs. They are all talking to each other as I just sit there, lost in my own thoughts. Melanie stands up and hands out self-defense books to every student.

"This book is illustrated, and it will show you the techniques that you will need to learn. This book is yours for the duration of the class, but it MUST be returned at the end of it. Failure to do so will result in a punishment, which is left up to Jaila. The other members have a vote too. More times than not though, she sways the vote in her favor. That doesn't mean if something accidentally happens to the book, that you'll be penalized. That only happens if you try to keep it or destroy it on purpose.

"As much as this is going to suck, this is how the remainder of the three weeks will go. The first half of the class will be spent in the gym. The second half will be spent in here, with the books. Once the three weeks are over, we will get into more exciting things. As I explained before, this is the only thing that we can do that will be taught and these teachings *can* leave the room. I cannot stress enough that once the three weeks are up, NOTHING can be shared that you are taught. If you feel the need to talk about what you are learning, talk to me or make a friend in the class. If you are caught selling, talking about, or even trying to teach what you learn here, you WILL be expelled and tossed into the radiation. This is not my call, but the council's. Thankfully we've never lost a student due to this behavior, because they've all heeded the warning. I suggest that you all do the same.

"Please, begin." She says, as she makes her way to her desk and goes on her tablet. Even though I know all of this already, I read it anyway because I know that I am supposed to.

Soon enough, but not nearly fast enough, the bell rings signaling the class is over and its dinner/leisure time. Thank god for that too. I was starving since I skipped breakfast and lunch.

Chapter Five

"So how was your first day?" Hazel asks me, as she eats her dinner.

"Where do I even begin?" I say as the days events replay in my mind. "First, you have to tell me all about your day with Annia in the caretaker class. Speaking of Annia, where is she?" I ask, looking around the room.

Hazel shrugs. "She said she'll be down later, that she had some things to do in her room. The class was amazing. I'm glad you made me sit in on it. It really seems like my calling. Thank you Jun. Plus I got paired up with a really cute boy, so all is well with the world." We both look at each other and burst out laughing. "Enough about my day, tell me about yours." She says to me.

"Well, I got to spar with Melanie today." I say, as Hazel's eyes grow wide. "I ended up knocking her out, then she congratulated me for it." I decided to leave her knowing my father and what happened between London and I out of it. I did not want to have to explain that right now.

Hazel's mouth hung open in shock. "Maybe I chose the wrong class." I roll my eyes at her, and she giggles. "Are there any cute boys in your class? God, there has to be. They must all be in pristine shape too if you guys are in the gym all the time training. I'm so jealous." She says. She is such a girl. "Do you have your eye on anyone?" She asks. My mind *automatically* sees London's face, and my cheeks feel warm.

"No." As I say it, I knew I said it a little too quickly.

Damn.

Again, her mouth drops. "You lie! You must tell me who he is!" She all but demanded.

I shake my head as I say, "No. I am not saying a word. I can't let myself think like that. You shouldn't be thinking about boys either. We need to focus on getting out of Discovery in one piece. Not to mention that we're still in the first week. Don't you think that is a bit quick?" I look around and lean in a little closer so no one can hear what I am about to tell her, and whisper, "I learned today that all of Discovery aside from the bathrooms and our rooms, are under surveillance. Be careful."

Her eyes grow wide in shock, her food stopped midair on the way to being eaten. "Are you serious?" She whispers back.

"Yes. Now please act like I told you something embarrassing, and not like I told you a huge secret." I whisper back forcing my cheeks to turn red, acting like I just admitted to something. Her eyes grow wide and her mouth drops open a bit, feigning shock. She leans in and says, "It's never too early to find someone attractive. Heck, some people know the minute they see each other. You never know. I apologize for this in advance." She says as she giggles.

She turns her head to look at me and says, "No way that happened! Do you know the name of the boy who pantsed you in the gym?!" She shouts. Everyone within hearing distance turned and looked at me. Forget my cheeks, my face was burning. Hazel smiled, and left hastily while laughing as she made herself lost in the crowd.

I will pay her back for that!

Suddenly, from behind me I feel two hands land gently on my shoulders. "Is that what you're telling people?" London whispers in my ear. I jump and turn around facing him, our faces mere inches apart. I am momentarily frozen in place. "I understand why you feel the way that you do. I do. I have to say that I am never as forward as I've been with you. I've only known you what, five minutes? Spoken to you what, another five minutes? I don't know why or what it is, but I feel drawn to you. It's almost overpowering. I'll give you your space, just know that I will not stop trying to get to know you Juniper." He says as he grabs my hand and kisses it gently before he walks away.

The hand he just kissed feels like it's on fire. I understand what he is saying though. I feel drawn to him as well. I've never been so attracted to someone almost instantly. When he is so close, it's like I can't move, can't think, can't breathe.

Once he is gone I can finally move again. I let out a breath that I hadn't known I was holding in. I didn't have to look around to know everyone was staring at me.

I could *feel* it.

Without looking at anyone, I got up, went up to my room and shut the door.

What the heck was wrong with me? Why does he affect me the way that he does? I can't believe I am letting him affect me so much. I've had boyfriends before. I've been on dates. It's not like I've never seen a boy. I've never gone all the way with one, but I have gone to second base with a boy.

I don't know why I'm feeling like this.

Get your head on straight Juniper.

It was almost time to go and meet up with Melanie, thank god. Lord knows I could use the distraction. I was nervous and excited at the same time. She knew my father. Maybe she knew why he just disappeared? Hopefully I was going to find out some long overdue answers tonight.

I got off of my bed and got myself together. I began to walk down the hallway. The anticipation was flowing through me. I felt alive and anxious at the same time. I couldn't wait to get there.

Melanie was already there when I got there, waiting for me in the furthest corner of the bathroom. She smiles warmly at me when she sees me coming to her.

"Hello Juniper. I can't believe I am meeting you. Terryn spoke very highly of you and your mother. He also told me that if he were caught, when you became of age, that I be the one to tell you what really happened to him. We don't have much time, but the first thing you should know is that he *is* alive."

My eyes grow wide with shock.

My father is still alive...

"You and your mother were led to believe he just left. That isn't the case. He uncovered a highly guarded secret. One of which, if he got caught, he would be killed on the spot or tossed into the radiation. He feared for you and your mother, so he came to me because he trusted me."

"You see, he was the enforcer that was tasked to keep the intelligence sector up to date on the happenings in the compound. This was a job that he could tell no one about. If the wrong people found out about what his secret job was, they could use it against him and/or feed him false information."

"During one of his patrols, he came upon two council members talking. He overheard them talking about the list of "sacrifices" in that year's Discovery group. He overheard them talking about the ones they felt were going serve no purpose, and the ones who would fight back against them. They were to have their results altered if they passed their classes, and they were to be thrown out into the radiation."

I just stood there for a second, mouth agape in shock. I could not believe what I was hearing. "Why would they be sacrificing kids every year?" I asked in utter disbelief, shock, and horror.

Melanie looked both ways to make sure no one was around, then she leaned in close so only I was able to hear her. "I personally think it is population control, to get rid of anyone they believed they couldn't control. Your father asked me to look into it, and that's what I got out of what I found."

"Your father was getting ready to expose what the council was up to. They found out before he could. He was given an ultimatum; forget what he had uncovered, or be tossed out. But if he chose to forget what he had uncovered, he would have had to tell them who it was that had helped him... He would have had to give me, and a few others up whom I had gotten to help us." She said, unable to look at me now. "He chose to be thrown out into the radiation rather than give up anyone. He knew if he had, they would have been tossed out along with him anyway. He saved many lives.

You see, the council has a way of getting what they want out of you. They promise you the world, then toss you out anyway." Her words laced with disgust.

I had no words.

I was speechless.

They killed innocent people and children to keep themselves fed. They killed those whom they thought would object to what they were doing... Those who would fight back. Those who dared to question...

I felt my stomach turn.

Then something that Melanie said came back almost knocking the air right out of me.

My father is *alive*.

"If my father was thrown out into the radiation, how do you know he survived?" I asked. My voice was distant, unbelievin and unwilling to get my hopes up for nothing. I mean, it had been three years...

"I'm in intelligence. We have spies inside and outside the compound. He got a message to me saying he was alive. He intended to put a stop to what the council did and when he had enough people to back him, he would come back for you and your mother." She said with sadness in her eyes. I don't need her pity. I needed my father, and he fucking *chose* to be thrown out of the compound!

All of this time, and he didn't think it would have been important to let his wife and child know that he was alive. He let us mourn him because we thought he was were dead?! To go through a funeral?! I was trying to understand, to bury the anger bubbling up inside me.

It was becoming increasingly difficult.

For a moment I couldn't speak. How could so many people survive the radiation? Did the council know that so many people survived the radiation? She must have seen my face, because she answered all the questions I couldn't ask at the moment.

"Your father is among the lucky ones to survive. A lot of people do not. The ones that do sometimes come out mutated. Your father, thankfully, did not." She said.

As she was speaking, I couldn't help myself. I felt the heat rise to my cheeks. She knew that he was alive, and didn't tell me or my mother? I don't care what my father said, that seems rather cruel to let us think he just left us.

"Why didn't you come to my mother or I to tell us that he was alive? We have spent the last three years believing that he just up and left us! Or worse, died! We even had a funeral for him because no would tell us what the fuck happened?! Didn't you think we deserved to know?!" I say, pissed the fuck off.

"I know it was cruel, but we had no other choice." She says firmly.

My eyes nearly pop out of my head. "No other choice?! How about coming to one of us to let us know that he was alive?!" I shout, throwing my hands in the air in frustration.

She looks at me, her face firm. "Do you honestly think that your father would let you both think that if there was any other choice? If word got back to you that he was alive and the council found out about it, it would have been assumed that you knew what was going on and you would have been cast out along with him! Along with the person that told you! Do you really think he could live with himself if he got you both tossed out, running the risk of killing you?! Whether you choose to believe me or him, is up to you. He was protecting the both of you!" She said, her voiced raised.

She began to pace while she spoke, and immediately I felt horrible. Of course he thought he was protecting us. I can't say that I wouldn't have done the same in his shoes.

"I'm sorry to dump all of this information on you and run, but we have been in here longer than it takes to use the bathroom." She warns. "We'll talk again. Hopefully by then you'll understand that it needed to be done." She says as she is about to leave.

"Wait!" I call out to her. She stops, and turns around. "I just wanted to say thank you." She gives me a questioning look. "I know I lost my cool, and I'm sorry for that. Thank you for telling me the truth. Thank you for telling me that he is alive. It's just so much to take in."

She smiles, "You're welcome, and I understand. I'll go first. Wait ten minutes, then go straight to your room." I nod, and she walks off into the hallway as I watch her until I can't see her anymore.

So now what do I do? I am left with all this new information. I just can't believe what she told me.

My father is alive...

My father is *alive*!

I can feel the tears beginning to pool in my eyes. All this time... All this time we thought he left us... We never thought he'd just leave us. But as time went on, and he didn't return...

We didn't know what to think.

I raised my hand and wiped the few tears that escaped away with the back of my hand.

Then on top of everything else, to have your suspicions about the council confirmed... I place my head in my hands and sigh loudly.

All of those innocent souls...

Sacrificed...

For no good fucking reason...

I feel my stomach begin to turn again, running to the nearest toilet to vomit.

I don't know how long I sat there with the new information just swirling around in my head, stewing. How could another human being do what the council was doing to other human beings? Have we learned nothing from our ancestors? Why do they have to be so heinous...? So many people killed... Just to protect themselves...

Oh god, my stomach... I grabbed the bowl and puked again. How did nobody see what was going on? Unless... Unless they got rid of anyone and everyone who they suspected knew...

I knew I had been in here too long. If they were watching me, they'd be suspicious. I got up, rinsed my mouth out and washed my hands. So many emotions were running through me at this moment.

I was happy that my father was still alive, and not mutated by the radiation.

I was very angry that the council was committing murder under everyone's nose and getting away with it.

Lastly, I was frustrated about what I can and can't do with the information that was just given to me.

I splash some cold water on my face, taking a deep breath in and out before I make my way out of the bathroom.

The walk back down to my room took longer than normal because I was walking so slow. I was still absorbing what was revealed to me tonight. You would think that we humans would have learned not to be so cruel to each other after the last great world war...

After so many died...

After we literally destroyed our world...

You would think we would have learned from our past! Why do we feel the need to harm one another in such ways!? For crying out loud, we have chased ourselves underground!

Things needed to change. I do not know how or when I'll be able to change things, but I will change them before I die. Even if it is the last thing that I do... I hope...

Chapter Six

I was too wired by the information I received to fall asleep. That was the night I learned the truth from Melanie. I ended up in the gym trying to work out my frustrations. I do not know how long I was in there. I do however, know that I only got a few hours of sleep before that god-awful alarm woke me up.

I groaned loudly at it, wishing death upon it.

A week had passed since that eye-opening night, and surprisingly I had been able to dodge everyone that was not in my class. I did not know how I could face my friends and not tell them the truth. I did not know how to warn them of the corrupt council, and their murderous intentions.

I inhaled deeply as I got up and got ready for my day. I was not sure how I was going to face anyone today knowing what I know. I know that one of them can be the next victim. It's how I felt every morning after she enlightened me with the truth. I'm going to need to talk with Melanie again today. I also knew that I couldn't dodge everyone forever. If I didn't see Hazel soon, I knew she'd come looking. No sooner had that thought crossed my mind, I ran into Hazel. She was waiting outside my class.

"Hey Jun, where have been? No one has seen you in over a we-are you okay?" I didn't know what to say to her, let alone what was even safe to say to her. I wanted to warn everyone, but

I knew that until I talked with Melanie again, I had to keep calm. So I decided to tell her half of the truth.

"Yeah Hazel, I am okay. I just haven't been sleeping well, and we have been learning so much in class. So if I seem cranky or out of the norm, that's why." I say as convincingly as I could. Hazel narrows her eyes at me. She can always tell when I am not telling her the truth.

"I know by the look on your face and by the way that you have been acting lately, that is a load of shit. You'll tell me when you're ready. Just remember, I am your friend and I am here for you. Although, you might want to work on your tells if you plan to be successful in Intelligence. No one should be able to read you like a book." She says.

I smile lightly at her, silently thanking her for dropping it, flipping her off for her smart-ass, but very true remarks. We part ways promising that we will meet up for lunch.

When I get into class I try my best not to stare at Melanie. I kept my distance from her, while I tried my best to digest what she has told me. I had to talk to her more about it now though, since my mind was a little clearer on the subject. She looked a little frazzled this morning though. I wondered what that's about. I know I have been dodging her, but that couldn't be the reason she was looking the way she was.

"Good morning everyone. I hope you got plenty of sleep last night. We have a long day of training ahead of us." She says as she makes her way to the door motioning us to follow her.

As we make our way to the gym, she hangs back. I decide to hang back too. "Good morning Juniper." She says as she casually slips something in my front pocket. "After dinner tonight. Same place, same time. Read that in your room beforehand." She whispers, before she casually makes her way back to the front of the class as we reach the gym.

"Everyone, listen up. Today we will be starting out with a cardio and strength workout. By the end of the week, I want to see you on the salmon ladder! London's class will be joining us for the workout. After the workout, both sexes will begin sparring with each other. Do not hold back. I know there are more guys in here than girls. Guys, do not hesitate to give your best in a fight because you are fighting a girl. In the real world, that can get you killed or seriously hurt."

"Did I hear somebody call my name?" London asks as he winks at me. In an instant, everyone is looking at me as they follow his gaze. My face is instantly hot. I am sure that will not help the rumors that are going to be spreading like wildfire. Jesus, what is wrong with him! Even Melanie gives me a sideward glance, trying to see if she missed something in a week. He smirks at my red face. I roll my eyes, red face and all, and look away.

I can feel all fifteen sets of eyes burning into me.

"I was just telling my trainees that you and your trainees will be joining us for our workout this morning. The sparring between both sexes will begin today." She says to him, taking everyone's attention off of me for the moment. I inhale sharply as I close my eyes, grateful for the distraction.

"Okay, first let's begin with some stretches." London says, as he stretches his arms over his body then bends forward, touching the floor. Melanie walks through the crowd, making her way to me.

"So, do you want to tell me what that was about?" She asks as she mimics London, stretching with me.

"It doesn't matter. I need to focus on getting out of here alive, not boys." I say as I copy the stretches that London is doing. Melanie gives me a questioning look.

"As long as you follow that, we will be okay. There will be plenty of time for boys once you graduate. We need you to be focused." She says lowly, sternly, and for the first time, actually sounding like my teacher.

This time it is me who gives her a questioning look. "That is my plan, but who is *we*?" I ask.

"That is in here." She says, as she casually touches her front pocket. A look of understanding passes across my face, as it dawns on me that she is referring to the note she slipped me earlier.

We finish up stretching, and Melanie makes her way back to the front of the class. "Alright everyone, we're going to do a different type of workout, one you've probably never have done before. It is a mixture of yoga and cardio. We blended it up, because it offers the best training for strength and flexibility when done correctly. Copy exactly as I do. If you need a break, or are unsure, either London or myself will help and show you any modifications that may be needed. Please do not try and tough it out. If you feel you need a few minutes or a modification, it is okay. You can hurt yourself and be thrown out, because you tried to be tough."

Melanie and London proceed to show the class how to breathe properly, how to keep everything tight as you work out. They made no fast movements, only slow and controlled ones.

I copy the movements, but my mind is not where it needs to be. It keeps wandering back to everything that I've learned, and what I'm going to learn. I couldn't stop thinking about it.Tonight. Tonight just couldn't come soon enough.

I bring my leg into a forward lunge, twisting my body, raising my hand in the air. As soon as I do I feel my ankle twist in a way that is not natural, as piercing pain shoots up through my ankle and foot.

"Fuck!" I shout as I fall down, catching my fall with my hands. Melanie looks over at me, concerned. She's about to come over, but London is up and over to me first. This can't be happening! I can't be taken out by a fucking stretch! This is unreal! I put my head in my hands, disgusted with myself.

"Focus is up here class." Melanie says as they all look over at me. At her command, they bring their focus back up to her. She however, is focused on us.

"Juniper, are you okay?" London asks, worry evident in his voice. I look up at him, and must have given him a look that could turn him into stone. "Is that look really necessary?" He asks, annoyed.

I roll my eyes. "No. I'm sorry, I twisted my ankle and it

hurts. I think I might have sprained it." I say, groaning a little at the throbbing.

"Let me take a look," He says, as he goes to inspect my leg. He places his fingers at the hem of the bottom of my left pant leg and raises it so he can assess my ankle. He touches it, and I flinch. When he sees me flinch he looks at me apologetically. "I'm sorry. I didn't mean to hurt you. Are you able to move your ankle?" He asks softly.

I raise my leg in an attempt to move it, which I do. As soon as I do though, shooting pain goes straight up my leg. "Ahhh! I can move it, but it really hurts to." I say, wincing at the pain.

"I'm sorry, but this is going to hurt. Tell me if it becomes too much, and you cannot take it." I smile tightly with my face scrunched in pain, as I nod my head yes. He takes his left hand and holds my leg in place. Then he takes his right hand, and uses it to move my ankle in circles. Immediately I am in pain, but not unbearable pain.

After about thirty seconds of that, he pushes my pant leg back down. "Your ankle is swollen. I think if you stay off it for a few days and keep it elevated, you will be just fine." I throw my head back and sigh. This is not what I need right now. London smirks at me, "Oh stop it, you'll be up and training in no time. You don't need to worry about falling behind either. You're way ahead of your classmates. Here, let me help you to your room." He says, as he offers his hand to me.

"No thank you London. I'll be escorting Juniper back to her room. Stay here and keep the workout going with the rest of the students." Melanie says as she walks back to us.

Thank god.

London looks at her, confused. "It's really no big deal." He says. "I wouldn't mind one bit."

She gives him a warning glance, which causes him to give her one. "She is my student, therefore, my responsibility."

"That wasn't an issue when I came over here to see if she was okay. Why are you acting this way?" He demanded. At this point Melanie looked completely annoyed.

"Back off now London, and drop it." She says so low that unless I saw London's reaction, I wouldn't have thought that she said anything. Visibly annoyed, he gets up.

"I'll check on you later." He says looking at me. "As for you, you owe me an explanation for whatever the fuck that was." He says to Melanie, visibly pissed off. "Alright class, eyes on me. Get ready to spar!" He demands.

Melanie bends down to help me up, throwing my arm over her shoulder. "Lean to the right, keep that leg elevated. Do not put any pressure on it. Okay?" She says. I nod at her, and we begin the now long trek back to my room.

The walk is relatively quiet back to my room. Now I understand why. I am almost glad that I sprained my ankle. Melanie will have a reason to be in my room, and we can talk some more.

I hope.

When we get to my room, she helps me into my bed placing a pillow under my left leg to help keep my foot elevated.

"I can't stay long. They will be expecting me back in the gym soon. Read the note I slipped to you earlier, I will be back after dinner." She says. I close my eyes and smile at her. Well, as much as I could muster one through the pain. "Is there anything you need before I leave? You really shouldn't get up and put weight on that foot if you don't have to."

"No, I think I will be okay. Thank you." I say a little disappointed that I will have to wait, still... I understood why though.

"Alright Juniper, see you soon." She says as she walks out the door. Once I am alone, I pull out the letter that she had slipped into my jeans earlier.

"Juniper,

They are onto us already. From this point on we have to be extremely careful. You CANNOT act on the information that I gave to you last week. You have to sit on it for now. If you go around throwing out accusations without any proof, it will be you who is thrown out. I'm not saying that you said a word. I'm just warning you. When I first found this out, I wanted to kill every last council member. If I had done that though, I would have been caught and killed before I could do anything about it, making lasting changes.

I wanted to let you know that your father and I do have a plan. He has gathered at least 75 people. Only ten of those people came out of the compound within the last five years. The other people, they came from people who were thrown out ages ago, and have bred. They have been trying to establish a community of sorts, but they could never seem to stay together long enough to settle. Your father has been able to unite them and he has them working together. He has been training them for about two years. We still need more people to take on the compound successfully though.

I have been trying to gather evidence to use against the council; of them saying what your father over heard all those years ago. I think that they have learned from the last time they were caught by Terryn. They have been extra careful.

Rip this letter to pieces and burn it. I'll see you tonight.

-M"

I'll rip up the letter, and I will give it back to her when she comes to check on me tonight. I won't be going anywhere. In a way it was almost a blessing that I sprained my ankle. Now she'll have a reason to come to my room. I still had so many questions.

A few hours go by and I hear a knock at my door. I'm slightly confused because I know it's not dinner time yet, so it couldn't be Melanie. At least I didn't think so.

"Jun, it's London. I know you can't get out of bed yet, and I thought you might be hungry. I brought you up some lunch. Do you mind if I bring it in?"

Shit... At his words, my stomach growls loudly. I hadn't noticed how hungry I was until he said something... "Come in

London."

He opens my door. London is holding some pizza and a few juices on a tray in his hands, along with a giant smile...

I am in trouble...

"Hey Juniper, how are you feeling?" He asks, as he shuts the door behind him, making his way over to my bed.

I smile back, grateful for his kind gesture. "It could be worse. It hurts, but I'll be fine. Nothing that I can't handle."

He smiles at that. "That I do not doubt." He says as he pulls a chair up to my bed. "I brought my lunch too, in hopes that you'll allow me the pleasure of eating my lunch with you?" He asks hopefully.

"Of course you can. You were nice enough to bring this to me after all. Just know that my view has not changed. I am not looking for any more than friends here while I'm in Discovery. I just cannot afford to be distracted, or risk getting attached to anyone. If they fail for some reason, or I fail because my focus was elsewhere... Just, no distractions."

He looks at me for a few minutes before he responds. "Well, I will respect your wishes. I can handle being friends first, getting to know you more. I'm just so confused as to why I am drawn to you the way that I am so soon. This has never happened to me before, with anyone. Maybe it's because you're the first person, guy or girl, who has come into these classes already knowing how to handle yourself. Or maybe it is the way that you carry yourself? I just don't know. I can't tell you how attracted I was to you when I saw you take down Melanie. But if friends are all you'll have right now, well, I'll take it then,won't I? You seem worth the wait." He says the last part with a giant sarcastic grin on his face. What an ass.

"*Seems* worth the wait?" I ask, equally sarcastic. He just chuckles as he eats his pizza.

"So tell me a little about yourself? Where are you from? Who are your parents?" He asks, genuinely curious.

"As you know, my father was an enforcer and my mother is a teacher. I believe this whole system is a piece of garbage and a cop-out, to feel better about killing a bunch of kids who don't fit the mold." I say the last part a bit nasty. I didn't mean it towards him, it's just the mere thought at what they do pisses me off.

He sits there for a moment mulling something over in his head. He looks at me astonished, somewhat guarded. Great, I must have scared him off with the way that I was talking.

"Well, I agree with you on that last part. I personally feel that they are just picking whom they think will be the easiest to control, tossing the rest out into the radiation, tests be damned." He says coldly.

I'm taken back a little by his admission. I haven't come across anyone other than Melanie, with the same thought. "So, tell me a little about yourself London?" I asked, now intrigued. He smiles lightly.

"What would you like to know?"

"Where are you from?"

"I am from the southern parts of the compound."

"What made you want to become an enforcer?" I asked this because I truly wanted to know. Out of all the things he could have been, he choose one of the toughest jobs there is in the compound. He takes a deep breath before he answers.

"If I am being completely honest... I have always wanted to be an enforcer. I've always looked up to them as our protectors. The ones you can count on. I love what I do, protecting people. Plus the uniform is kinda cool." He says, showing off his uniform. Full of yourself much? I just roll my eyes at him. "What? You can't say it's not." He says as he smirks. *Oh yeah*, definitely full of himself, I say to myself as I chuckle to myself.

"Do you regret your decision?"

"Not for a second. I've met some of my dearest friends here." He says confidently. "Can I ask you something else?"

"Sure, but if it's too personal, I might not answer it yet." I say to him being completely honest. As nice as he is, I do not completely trust him yet.

"Fair enough. Why did you choose to be in intelligence? Why not an enforcer like your dad, or a teacher like your mom?"

He asks sounding generally interested.

"As admirable as being a teacher is, I would not be able to handle all of those children at once. Growing up with having my mother as a teacher has taught me that you really have to have a passion for teaching. If not, you end up hating it and that effects everyone around you. As far as my father goes, I really can't get into too much of it without giving too much away. The only thing I will say of it is, that it hurts too much to even think of becoming an enforcer..." I say the end of it with such sadness that there is no way that he didn't pick up on it.

His eyebrows furrow together deep in thought. "Your father wasn't killed was he?" My eyes look up at him, tears threatening to spill over almost giving me away. "I'm so sorry Jun, you do not have to answer if you don't want to." He says with a sadness in his voice.

I take a second to compose myself with a nice, long, deep breath. I place my hand on his thigh as I say, "It's okay. No, he wasn't killed. That's all I am going to say on the matter." London just shakes his head yes, concern written all over his face.

He places his hand on mine as he says, "Until you're ready to talk to me about your father, I will never bring it up again. On this, you have my word."

I smile lightly at him. "Thank you."

"Okay, before things get too heavy in here, I think I'll take my leave. The alarm should be going off any minute now for classes to begin again." As soon as he says that, it blares.

We both wince at the sound.

"You never get used to that." He says. "Thank you for a lovely lunch. Dare I ask if we can do this again tomorrow?" He asks, our hands still touching...

On his thigh...

His very muscular thigh...

"I'd like that very much. Thank you for this, and thank you for coming to check on me." As I motion towards the empty trays, and to us.

"No problem, you're more than welcome. Keep your foot

elevated and please try not to walk on it. See you tomorrow." He says as he walks towards my door.

"See you tomorrow." I say as he is closing the door.

Chapter Seven

I must have fallen asleep because I woke up to the alarm going off, signaling the end of the day. As I am forced to lay here, I can't help but think of him. London is everywhere. That was nice of him to bring me lunch and keep me company. He is attractive physically, yes. What matters more to me is the way he is, the way he carries himself, and how he treats others. So far he has shown me that he is a wonderful person. He is someone that I can see myself with when this is all over...If I make it through Discovery that is...

As much as I try to will it away, I can't help the way my heart beats when I think of our lunch date tomorrow.

Did I just say *date*?

Good god woman.

It's not a *date*.

I also have to remind myself of the warning that Melanie gave me, *'they're onto us already.'* I would never be able to forgive myself if something happened to him because we got too close.

There is a knock at my door, which I am thankful for. I need to get London off of my mind.

"Hey Juniper, how are you feeling?" Melanie asks as she comes in carrying food.

"I'm okay." I say.

"It's almost a good thing that you hurt your ankle, it gives us time to talk in here without it looking suspicious." She says, as she sits down next to my bed. "I brought you some grilled cheese and tomato soup. I hope that is okay."

I smile gratefully. "That's good, thank you." I say to her as she hands me the food. "Not to jump right into business, but how do you know that the council is onto us already?"

She walks over to my door. She opens it, looking both ways before she shuts it and locks it behind her. She makes her way back over to me, pulling the chair a little closer to my bed.

"Do you remember how I said that we're constantly being watched, except in our dorms and in the bathrooms?" She asks very quietly, almost at a whisper. I nod. "Well, it seems that we were seen going into the bathroom together, and when I left it took you almost twenty minutes to leave. I heard from a friend that they overheard key members in the council talking about it. When they saw that, they looked over the tapes from the day before. They looked at all of our interactions. To put in frankly, they know that I knew your father. Now, they are going to be keeping a much closer eye on the both of us."

"It's my fault. I should've been more discreet when I realized who you were. I should have never said anything about anything out in the open the way that I did." She says it full of remorse.

"It's fine. They probably have been watching my every move anyway. They know exactly who I am. So, that leaves the bigger question, what are we to do from here? Is there anyone we can trust, anyone who can help?"

"I have an idea of one other person that I can trust right now. I really do not want to bring any more people into this if I do not have to. Not even for the fact of trust, but for the liability. I do not want anyone to have to make the same sacrifice that your father did."

The sacrifice... I have to remind myself why he did what he did. He did it for a good cause. That is the only way that I can't hate him for abandoning us with no reason why for thinking, and believing that he was dead would be better for us.

"So what do you know of what he found? Have you been able to come up with any solid proof?"

"At this moment all we have is the word of others, nothing concrete. You have to remember the fear that is instilled in people as children. No one wants to get caught spying on them for fear of their own, and their families lives."

I stare at her in shock for a moment, trying to comprehend what she just told me. "So you're saying that in the three years since my father was tossed out, there really hasn't been anything new found out? Nothing concrete??" I asked in utter disbelief.

"Sadly, no. Nothing concrete. Like I said, just whispers and hearsay."

"Okay, so what do you have planned? How do you plan on getting this said information?"

"Do you remember when I said you have to be ready for anything? Well, in intelligence not only do you have to be ready physically, you also have to be prepared mentally. That means patience. Once you graduate you'll have a security clearance, and you will be able to get into rooms that only we have access to. In those rooms we will be able to go into greater lengths and more detail.

"If I had been more careful about it in the beginning, we could have talked more about it. Now we have to be extremely careful. I will continue to check in on you, but we need to have a more teacher/student relationship when there are eyes on us."

Is she high?

"You expect me to sit on this for six months? All of this new information, and I can't say a thing or try to learn anything new?" I ask in disbelief.

She speaks to me with an apologetic tone, "Look, I'm sorry, but yes. You can think of it as extra training that the other students will not get."

My mouth dropped open in shock. "This isn't hypothetical situations. This is my family, and the fact that they are blatantly murdering people and getting away with it... I really have no idea how you sat on it this long." I say as calmly as I can, trying to keep the anger at bay. I could tell Melanie was losing her cool, but was she serious?! How could she expect me to do that?!

"Okay hot shot, how are you going to get intel? You or I, we're not allowed to leave Discovery. How are you going to sneak around and get the evidence that you need? Are you trying to get us caught? What do you think will happen to you if you go around pointing fingers with no evidence to back it up? What do you think will happen to your mother? We have to play this smart Juniper. I know that you're smarter than the way you're thinking right now. I know it's the shock and anger talking. She scoots a little closer to me, placing a hand on each of my shoulders. As she does this, I begin to understand what she is saying. I knew she was right about me not thinking clearly, and about me needing to be smart about it.

"You are going to promise me that you will not act on it. At this point, you'd be getting us both tossed out." I never seen such fear in her eyes. It was that moment I knew I had to trust her.

"I don't like it one bit, but I will do as you ask. What am I to do now?"

"Be like every other student in Discovery. Make friends, do your work, hit the gym. The opportunities are endless." She smirks as she stands.

"You're hilarious." I say with as little enthusiasm as I could muster.

"See you tomorrow Juniper. I'll check on you after dinner again tomorrow unless you need me beforehand?"

I try to hide the small amount of blush that creeps up on my face, but I can't and she sees it. Disappointment crosses her features. "I know I can't tell you what to do, and you already know my feelings on the matter. Just be careful. I care for London, and I do not want to drag him in on this." This time I give her a questioning look full of insinuation. "It's nothing like that Jun, he is like a little brother to me."

"It's nothing like that for me either. I told him that all I am looking for is friendship while I am in here. I'm not going to lie and say that I don't find him attractive. But I am not going to act on that either. Not now, not with so much at risk."

"All I am saying is that things happen. We have little control over it sometimes, no matter how hard we try. I've seen the way he looks at you, and the way you look at him. It's not just a normal 'I'm checking you out because your hot kinda look.' Just play it safe. Be friends first, and once you get out of Discovery, take it from there. I'm not your mother, and if it happens beforehand, all I am asking is that you play it safe." She all but pleads.

"Okay, I will." I say it just to ease her mind. There was no way I was going to let that happen. Not when there was so much going on and so much to do. Melanie smiled at me, then left. There was so much to think about. Could I really just act like a normal student given all that I know? Could I really? I'm going to have to.

Chapter Eight

I slept horribly last night. It didn't help that I didn't have to go to the bathroom until this morning, when everyone else was sleeping. It was a comical sight to behold, watching me trying to get out of bed, then proceed to hop down the hallway to the bathrooms. Luckily for me, Hazel saw me on the way back to my room and helped me back into my bed. She then spent fifteen minutes bitching about how they should have someone to come and check on me every few hours if I'm supposed to be off of my feet completely. She offered to do it, but I told her that London and Melanie come to see me during lunch and dinner. She wouldn't leave until I let her come with breakfast. I personally felt as though she was making too much of it. I thought that they all were to be honest, it was just a sprain. It's not like I broke it or something.

Once I was settled in, she left to bring us up some breakfast. When she returned, we sat and talked about nothing in particular. We talked until the first alarm rang. How I hated that god awful alarm. I could feel it in my teeth every time it went off. We said our goodbyes with her promising to visit me at the end of the day.

Sitting in this bed all morning and most of the day yesterday, was killing me. I was beyond bored, and I slept to pass the time. I would have read, but like an ass I didn't bring any books. I guess I thought that I wouldn't be reading for my own pleasure while I was in Discovery. Because of this, my mind was all over the place.

In the span of a few weeks, I have learned so many things. Many of those things I just could not wrap my head around. The biggest thing though, was that my father was still alive. It felt so cruel that I couldn't tell my mother. Devastated is not even the word. If she knew he was alive, she would be so happy. Well, first she'd be happy, then angry for the same reasons that I was. She'd understand why like I did though. But, I also know she'd try to find a way out to be with him.

Unless….

No, she couldn't have known.. Could she? From the way she was talking about or hinting at the fact she has seen people topside, almost sounds as if she… No, she would have told me. I hope…

Only…

No…

If my father has been above ground living in the radiation all of this time…

She more less told me that she had seen the people above ground. She even looked around before she barely even whispered it to me. Could she have really figured it out and *seen* him? Did she hear from those on the outside that he was out there? If that was the case, then how didn't intelligence know about it? If they did, how'd Melanie not know about it? I'm going to have to talk to Melanie again about that this evening when I see her.

Knock knock knock. That must be London. Wow, is it lunchtime already? "Come in!" I shout so he could hear me.

He walks in with a bright smile on his face, carrying two trays of food. He places mine on my lap. London sits down on the nearby chair, moving it closer to my bed as he sits placing his tray on his lap.

"I got us potato stew today. I hope that's okay?"

"It is London, thank you." I say returning the smile.

"How are you feeling today? Can I get you anything?" He asks sweetly.

"No, this is fine. I'm okay. My ankle is just a little sore. How are you? How is the sparring going?"

He chuckles, "It's going. Some are better than others. I am only concerned with a couple of people. No one is as good as you though. However, I think I could give you a run for your money."

I roll my eyes at that statement. "That's doubtful."

"Is that so? I think I hear a challenge in that tone. Care to back that statement up when you're healed?" He asks, intrigued.

"I guess that was, wasn't it? Well sir, I think we'll have to spar when I am healed." I chuckled.

"First off, don't call me sir. Second, I accept your challenge." He says smirking as he eats his stew.

"This is nice, Jun." He says as he looks at me.

"What's nice?" I ask him, curious.

"Being able to sit here and talk, getting to know one another more without all the eyes." He says as a smirk plays on his face.

I return the smile because he is right. "It is, isn't it?"

We sat a few minutes in silence as we ate. It was a comfortable silence. It was quite refreshing.

"London, just out of curiosity, why out all the people here past and present, why am I the one you're pursuing? I told you that it would never happen while we are in here." I asked, because I was genuinely curious. He licked his lips with that damned cocky smile of his before he spoke. I truly think that he is doing that on purpose now...

"We're mighty confident in ourselves now aren't we?" He chuckles.

"Well yeah, have you seen me? I'm the total goddamn package." I tease.

"Don't I know it." He whispers to himself as his left eyebrow raises, finishing his last bite of soup. I feel bad then, because I know this can't go anywhere now. No matter how much I want it to the more I get to know him.

We both feel the uneasiness that crept up with what he said. Neither of us spoke on it. I know I caused this, and I feel bad for saying anything. I need to learn not to say the first thing that pops into my head... London could barely look at me. After a few awkward minutes, he finally looks up at me placing his hands on my bed.

"I'm sorry. I shouldn't have said that out loud. I know you told me how you feel, and I meant what I said when I said that I would give you your space on that. I promise to be more mindful of my comments. Forgive me?"

"Well how could I say no to an apology like that? I'm sorry too, I shouldn't have said what I said."

He smiles back just as the alarm sounds that lunch is over. We both wince at the sound.

"You never get used to that, and you don't have to apologize." He says as he stands, collecting both of our trays. "Same time tomorrow?"

I smile at him, "I look forward to it."

I'm not sure how much time passed but staring at these walls, it seemed like forever. Not to mention that I knew in a few short hours, I would be talking to Melanie again. I had so many more questions for her now.

Could my mother really have known?

If she did, how could Melanie not have known?

This is going to drive me crazy. I'm going to be just sitting here and dwelling, thinking of the what ifs. I have got to find something to do. As if on cue, there was a knock at my door. I wondered who that could be? It was nowhere near dinner time yet.

"Come in!" I shout.

A woman with jet black hair that was pulled back, wearing black slacks and a white top walked, into my room. I'd never seen her before. She walked right up to my bed and introduced herself. With her hand stretched out to shake mine, and a big smile placed on her face she says, "Hello Juniper, it's very nice to finally meet you. I'm Jaila."

To say that I was taken back a little, would be an understatement. We had to learn all the names of the council members, but unless they met with you or you were related, you never saw them as kids. You never knew what they looked like.

After that thought passed, I was instantly filled with rage. This is the fucking woman who is responsible for sending us out into the radiation if we so much as sneezed the wrong way.

Control yourself Juniper. Don't make it easier on her to get rid of you.

You can do this.

Remember the reasons why you need to stay in the compound. I accepted her hand into mine and shook it. "Hello Jaila." I say a little hesitantly. What the hell she could want?

Stay cool Juniper.

S t a y   c o o l.

"I heard of your most unfortunate accident during class, and I was wondering how you were holding up?" Dear god, how fake she was. I could see right through her facade.

"I'm okay. Friends check on me, and bring me food." I say just as fake as her concern for me was.

"Ah yes, your instructor is one of them right? How do you like Melanie? Do you feel she is doing a good job? Do you wish you had a different instructor?"

What the hell is she getting at? What is she fishing for?

"I think Melanie is an excellent teacher. So no, I wouldn't want another one. Why do you ask?" I ask as evenly as I can. My heart was pounding so hard that I can feel it in my ears. Staying calm is getting harder and harder by the second.

"I ask all the new students in Discovery this. I like to meet with all of the students, and I get their opinions on their instructors. I started with you today.

"You know, I knew your father well. It really is a shame what happened to him. It's an even bigger shame that no one ever found out what happened to him. You have my condolences."

What the fuck?

Is she serious?

She knows something, or she is trying to fish something out of me. She is probably one of the ones who confronted Melanie. Just to be safe, I don't even bother to acknowledge the last statement. I'm not going to let her bait me.

"Well, I have given you what you came in here for. Is there anything else you need?" She gives me a cocky smirk.

"Not at the moment. I just wanted to remind you that we all play by the rules here. Those who don't... Well, we all know what happens to those who don't. You should know more than others." She says that almost laughing.

It takes everything in me not to leap off of my bed and attack her. She knows what she is doing. She is trying to bait me and get under my skin. She's trying to get the better of me, trying to get me to turn on my friends.

Breathe Juniper, breathe. Don't give in to your anger. You can't change a thing if you're thrown out. Don't give her what she wants. You'll get your shot at her.

YOU WILL GET YOUR SHOT.

I won't give her the satisfaction.

She smiles at my silence as she walks towards the door. As she places her hand on the door knob, she turns back to me. "You should feel honored, not everyone gets a warning like you just got. They're simply taken care of immediately as to not start trouble within the compound. But, being that you cannot leave Discovery for another five and a half months, I have decided to be merciful and give you that time to reflect on how you wish your life to turn out. I adore your mother. I'd hate to have to break her heart, *again*."

She says the last part as she is closing my door. As soon as the door is shut, I bury my face in my pillows and scream. The anger I feel is radiating through my body. What the fuck was that? It must be nice to be able to just throw your weight around like that. Ohh I am going to enjoy bringing that narcissistic bitch down.

I try my damnedest to stay in bed, but I can't. Even though I am limping, I pace the floor. I wasn't sure if she was directly involved in my father's disappearance before, but I'm certain of it now. I wish dinner time would come faster then it was. I needed to talk to Melanie badly.

Knock knock knock. What's with all the surprise visits today? "Who is it?" I shout so I am not so taken off guard again.

"It's Annia. I was just coming by to see how you were."

Well I'll be! I haven't heard from her or seen her, since that day we toured classes. "Come on in."

Annia smiles softly at me as she opens the door. "I'm sorry that I haven't been around, I've just thrown myself into my studies. I want to be the best I can be, you know? To better my chances. Wait. What are you doing out of bed? Aren't you supposed to be off of your ankle?" She asks as she walks up to me.

"I don't think you have anything to worry about there. I know I'm just a little on edge. You'll never guess who was just in here. Jaila Montrose." I say as evenly as I could.

"Seriously? What did she want?"

"She said that she wanted to see how I was, and see how my class was going. She said that she was going to be asking all the students this, and that I was her first." I say to her, opting to not tell her the real reason why she was here. Melanie was right, the fewer people to know the better. I couldn't put people in harm's way for no reason.

"Here, let me help you to your bed. You really shouldn't be on it right now. You'll only hurt your ankle more, and possibly cause yourself to be out of classes even longer." She says as she gently grabs hold of my arm. I don't say anything because I knew that she is right.

I can start to feel the pressure on my ankle the second I am off my feet. I can't let Jaila get to me like that. I needed to pull myself together.

"I guess all the rooms look the same huh?" She asks. She asks it in more of a statement than a question.

"Yeah. Hazel's room looks the same way too." I say to her.

Annia spots the photo on my nightstand and picks it up. "Is this your family? I'm surprised you have a photo. They cost a lot of credits being as they're so difficult to make, since the end of the surface world came to be."

"Yeah, we were lucky. The photographer owed my dad a favor."

"Must have been a big favor." She says as she places the photo down. As she says that, the bell rings signaling the end of classes for the day. Thank god. That means Melanie will be here soon.

"I hate that bell." Annia says in full disgust. We both laugh at her reaction.

"You and I both." I chuckle.

"I'm going to go. I'm starving. Do you have someone to come and bring you dinner? If not, I can bring you a tray up if you'd like." She asks.

"I do. Thank you. Please stop by again though if you find the time. It gets lonely up here by myself all of the time."

She smiles, "I definitely will. As I said earlier, I've been diving into my studies. I hope you get well soon Jun." She says giving me a hug. "Take care of yourself."

"You too." I say as the door closes behind her.

Not much sooner than Annia leaves, Melanie walks in with two trays of food.

"Hello Juniper. How's your ankle today?" She asks as she makes her way to me.

"It's a little swollen, and it's completely my fault." I say as Melanie places the trays down. The facade I had up for Jaila and Annia falls, and Melanie can see the worry on my face.

"What happened?" She asks firmly, the worry was now evident in her voice.

I take a deep breath to calm my nerves before I speak. "I had a visitor today."

"From whom?" She asks, but she already knows the answer to that question.

"Jaila." I said it flatly. I see panic slightly cross Melanie's face as she stands.

"What did she want?"

"At first it was to see how I was doing, to see how my class was coming along and how I like my instructor. She claimed she does this with every student."

"She does. Why do I get the feeling that there is more to this?"

"Because there is. She more or less threatened me. She didn't come right out and say it, but I know she had a hand in my father's expulsion from the compound. She more or less told me that I need to focus on my studies, and to stop trying to find out what happened to my dad. That everyone here plays by the rules, and those that didn't get tossed out. She said that she'd hate to break my mother's heart *again*." As I am saying this, Melanie is pacing the floor.

"Did she say anything else?" She asks in full agent mode now.

"No."

Melanie stops pacing and walks over to me. "Now that it is confirmed that she knows we know something, we need to be even more careful than we have been. After today, I will not be coming back in here." She sees me try and interrupt her, but she raises her hand up to stop me. "I know you don't like the sound of that, but our lives now depend on it. The only time you will see me is during class, for which I have no doubt you will do well. Once you graduate from Discovery, we will bring this compound and the council to their knees." She says fiercely.

"I must go now, but I will make sure that someone is available to bring you dinner. Even though your ankle is a bit swollen, you should be good in a few days. Be careful Juniper." She says as she leaves.

"What the fuck?!" How the hell am I supposed to act as if things are just fine? I know I have to, but what the fuck? I cannot wait to bring this woman down, and this fucking council down. These people are going to feel every ounce of rage I have for them, and this godforsaken place.

Chapter Nine

I got no sleep again for the next few days. All I could do was stew on everything that happened. Stew I did. I thought of all the ways I could take Jaila and the council down. I thought on it so much, that I could actually feel the imaginary victory in my bones. It felt *good*. When I saw London and Hazel, I tried to act as if nothing was bothering me. Both of them saw right through me and could tell. They tried to get it out of me, but I refused to get them involved. I saw Annia again yesterday but she was in and out, just checking up on me.

True to Melanie's word, she had a classmate come up to bring me dinner the past few nights. His name was Ira. He seemed nice enough. We would have idle chit chat while we ate. Once I was done eating though, he would leave whether the bell rang or not. It didn't matter if he was done eating or not. I'm not sure if that was Melanie's instruction or his choice, but he did it every time.

After Ira left tonight, I decided to test out my ankle. It felt strong enough, but I needed to get some weight on it. I gently swung my legs off of my bed and onto the floor. I opted out of putting my shoes on and walked around my room. It was a little tender. However, I believed that was due to staying off of it for so long. After a few minutes of walking around my room, the tenderness in my ankle seemed to disappear. I decided to walk down the hall to test it some more, and build up some strength. I walked over to my closet to put on my sneakers before walking out of my room.

I managed just fine on my walk to the bathrooms, so I decided to take the walk further to the gym. Classes are out now, so it should be empty. Somehow I managed to make it to the gym without running into anyone. They all looked as though they were on the first floor.

When I entered the gym, a sense of belonging washed over me. Thankfully, as far as I could tell, there was no one else in here. I guess it couldn't hurt to do a little light training. I walked over to the punching bags and began throwing light jabs into it. Man this feels so good. This is exactly what I needed to relieve some stress. I add a few kicks, being wary of my ankle. The longer I go, the better my ankle felt. I amp it up a little. I was punching and kicking it harder. I'd imagine Jaila's face is on the punching bag, and I go to town.

Left, right, left, right, dodge, kick, dodge, jab! I yell in my head. The sound the punching bag makes as I hit it is music to my ears. I loved being in here. This is where I felt at peace. Just me and the bag. After about twenty minutes on the bag, I stopped and looked at the salmon ladders behind me.

Should I?

I jump up and down, to test how my ankle could handle the impact if I had to jump down. It's a bit sore, but it seems okay.

Fuck it. I decided I was going to try it.

With a cocky grin of my own, anticipation runs through me. I've always wanted to try this, but I've never been brave enough to. They had one in a recreation room near my mother's and I's apartment. I've seen many try and fail to climb it. I figured while no one was here to see if I fell or did it wrong, that there would be no one here to point and laugh.

I walk over to it and place myself just underneath it. I take a breath in and a breath out to calm myself. You can do this Juniper. I jump up and grab hold of the bar. I stay there for a moment swinging gently, enjoying the quiet. After a moment, I swing my body gently and use that force to propel my body into the jump, using my arms to the next set of hooks. The sound of the bar banging onto them sends excitement throughout my whole body.

Fuck yes!

With each passing hook that I rise up on the salmon ladder, pride and happiness runs rampant through my body. On the last hook, I can definitely feel it in my arms. I adjust my grip as I prepare to make my way back down the ladder. One by one, I make my way down to the last set of hooks. Once I reach them, I hop down because I feel like my arms are on fire and are going to fall off.

I shake my arms out and yell, "Hell Yes!" I felt amazing and accomplished. This was a high that I never wanted to come down from.

Clap, clap, clap, clap, clap!

Who the fuck was that? I could feel my heart pounding so hard that I could swear it was going to pound right out of my chest. No sooner than I ask myself that question, I see none other than London walking towards me.

Great.

"Jun, that was amazing! I see that your ankle is doing much better." He says with a smile.

"Thank you, it is. Why are you in here?" I ask trying to hide the blush creeping up in my cheeks.

"I always come in here after dinner to get in a late-night workout." He says as he grins. "Have you ever done that before?"

"No. I've always been afraid to try it. The one that was in the recreation center near my apartment; hardly anyone could do. But I figured I would give it a try while no one was in here to see me fail if I did. Totally failed there."

He rolls his eyes at the last statement. "From the way you just smashed that, I would have never known. Is there anything that you can't do?"

Hopefully he will attribute the blush creeping on my

cheeks to the workout that I just did, and not to the fact that he is in here shirtless with gym slacks on.

"So do you always work out shirtless, or do you like showing off for the ladies that might be in here after hours?" I tease.

A giant shit eating grin spreads across his face. "Is this making you uncomfortable Juniper?" He says as he flexes his chest and abs.

That motherfucker. *Holy shit*.

I bounce up and down shaking my head, trying to clear it to no avail. "How about I take you up on that challenge? Unless you're too scared to get your ass handed to you by a girl?" I tease as I take my stance.

He chuckles as he gets into his. "If you think you're ready to take this on," he says as he points to the length of his body, "then bring it." God damn it. I am going to have to focus.

"Don't you dare take it easy it on me just cause I'm a girl." There he goes again with that cocky fucking grin.

"Oh Jun, I have no intentions to." He says as he begins circling me. I throw my hands up and begin the dance.

I wait for him to make the first move, which he does. He steps in to throw in a quick jab, which I dodge effortlessly. He comes in again with a jab to my rib cage, but I block it. I watch his feet, his stance, and his hands. By doing this, I can anticipate what his next move will be. At least I hoped so.

As I am studying him, he is doing the same to me. He's watching every movie I make. This time I decided to throw in a couple of jabs, which he dodges, then immediately counters. Left, right, left, right, left, left. He comes at me jabbing into my arms, which are blocking my sides. Then he swoops down so fast that I didn't even see him sweeping his left leg under my right leg, knocking me down. In that moment, I am truly embarrassed that he got me with that move. I need to be more focused on what's happening then, instead of the lack of his shirt and taught muscles. I jump up to my feet just as fast as I fell.

"What's the matter Jun? Are you giving me freebies?" He

says smirking.

"You got lucky. That won't happen again."

And it fucking won't.

I move in again with a jab to his chest. Mother fucker catches my arm, and tries to bend it back. I quickly take advantage of this position and bring my knee into his rib cage, hard. He lets go, gasping for air as I pull myself together. He is back too in an instant with what looks like, excitement?

"Alright, now we're getting somewhere. Bring it Jun. Give me what you've got." He says, as he raises his hands defensively. I smile at that statement.

"Is that a cocky grin on your face?" He says, now teasing me.

My smile grows.

"Be careful what you wish for." I say.

We circle each other for a moment, like a beautiful dance trying to anticipate the others next move. That only lasts for a moment as he engages me throwing jab after jab, adding in a few kicks. I'm able to dodge and block every move he makes. I counter with a few jabs to his ribs myself, and catch him with an uppercut to that handsome face. It knocks him back, and he stumbles his footing. I take that opportunity to give him a roundhouse kick to chest, effectively knocking him to the ground. I stand there for a moment, gloating to myself that I just knocked him down.

He lays there for a moment trying to catch his breath. As I walk over to him, I instantly regret it. As my feet get in range of his, he side swipes my calf sending me to the floor. As soon as I hit the floor he pins my hands above my head, wrapping his legs around mine, completely immobilizing me. I try to free myself, but I am no match against his brute strength.

"Should've never let your guard down Jun! *That's* rule number one." He says it with a shit eating grin on his face. I roll my eyes at him because I know he's right.

He fucking got me.

Fuck.

After a minute though, we realize just how close we are to one another.

You could cut that tension with a knife.

My heart begins to beat harder, and I notice every little detail of the man hovering over me.

The sweat that has built up is now dripping down his taught muscles. His eyes are just staring at me, fighting with himself. The tattoos on his arms that are holding my hands above my head...

His lips all but calling my name...

In the back of my mind I can hear the rational Juniper saying to stop this, saying push him off. Saying to herself, *think straight*! When I am this close to him, all that rationality disappears. I can't even say his name. I attempt to, but all that comes out is a shaky breath that I didn't even know I was holding. I lick my lips and stare at his. I can feel my heart pounding harder with each passing second.

The second I look him in the eye his resolve crumbles, and he crashes his lips to mine. My hands and legs release in the process. Automatically, my hands wrap around his head, weaving my fingers through his hair, pulling him deeper into the kiss. Again, I can faintly hear the rational Juniper in the back of my mind. In this moment though, I don't care. All I can taste, sense, and feel is London. I feel his weight above me, his lips on mine, his hands on my face and neck, caressing me.

And damn it felt good.

So damn good.

It felt so good I parted his lips with my tongue, and deepened the kiss even further. This kiss was filled with passion, want, need, and desire. My hands traveled freely down the back of his neck, to his back, and I pull him closer to me. I don't know what has come over me, but I couldn't stop myself. Nor did I want to. I hear him moan ever so slightly, which only makes me pull him closer.

My doing that must have given him the courage to allow his hands to wander as he pulls us both up, still kissing. London places me on his lap, so that my legs are on either side of him. He runs his hands down my back to my ass, giving it a nice squeeze. which sends a shiver down my spine. Instinctively, my hips rock on his lap as his name escapes my lips. His lips leave my lips as he gasps slightly, beginning to kiss down the side of my face and down my neck. Then he brings his hands up my sides and past my chest, caressing my neck before placing each hand on my face pulling his lips back to mine, sinking deeper into the kiss.

My god this felt amazing; every touch, every kiss. At this point our hips were rocking with each other, and suddenly I could *feel* him.

It broke the daze I was in and cleared my head in an instant. This could not happen. Not now, and not here. I pushed London back and stood up.

The spell was broken...

The hurt in his eyes said it all. Stupid, stupid, stupid!

"I'm sorry London. I can't." I barely got out before I turned to run out of the gym. I heard him call after me, but I kept running.

What the fuck the is the matter with you! How could you let it go that far?! You know you can't get involved with him now. Not with so much at stake! This isn't fucking fair to me or to London! I can't play this game! Damn this fucking compound! What I wouldn't give to not know the things that I know. Maybe then I'd be able to let myself go and enjoy it here. Enjoy London... I reach my door and slam it shut once I'm inside. I run to my bed and scream into my pillow in frustration. Not even a second goes by when I hear my door open and close again. I look up, and to no surprise I see London.

He is fuming.

I can't say that I blame him.

"You know, at first I was sorry that I initiated the kiss after you jumped up and ran away from me. But you know what? I'm not now. You were into that kiss just as much as I was! What the fuck Juniper? I gave you your space. I was respectful. Then you kissed me back with so much *force*, so much *passion*, and I was so goddamn happy. I really, really, like you Juniper. I am not into playing games though. I don't know what you're looking for from me, but kissing me like *that*, then running full speed away from me? What is wrong with me? What did I do to you?!" He screams the last part, causing me to flinch back a little. He is right, he didn't deserve that. I let it get way out of hand knowing what I can and can't have right now. There was nothing wrong with him. It was all me.

With tears in my eyes, I look at him. When he sees the tears on the verge of falling, he immediately softens his stance, and closes the distance between us. He embraces me, and holds me as I cry. At first, I am crying for what happened between us. Then it's like the flood gates opened, and I let out all of the pent-up emotions that I have been trying to push aside out. He looks down at me with tears in his own eyes, pleading with me to tell him what's wrong.

Should I tell him?

Don't be stupid. You've been stupid enough for one night. The more he looks at me with those eyes, the harder it is not to say anything. He brings the back of his right hand over my cheek, caressing it softly.

"I don't know what you're afraid of, but you have no reason to fear me. You can trust me Juniper. Talk to me. *Please*." He pleads.

I push him back and walk towards my desk. I can see the hurt on his face again. I hate that I'm the one the that keeps putting it there. He didn't deserve any of this.

"You don't understand. It's not you. I really like you and I'm sorry I let things get out of hand at the gym." I say through the tears.

"If you really like me, and I really like you, then what is the problem?" He asks throwing his hands in the air, frustrated.

"So many things are riding on me having a clear mind. I can't get sidetracked, and I can't endanger people." I choke out. Confusion flashes across London's face at the last statement.

"How would you put anyone in danger? And as far as

getting sidetracked, you are so far ahead of your class in just the first month! You're practically a shoe in!"

"You don't understand!" I say as I raise my voice.

"Then help me understand! Help me understand why two people who really like each other can't be together?" He says a little more calmly. I want to tell him so bad, but every fiber of my being is telling me not to. But at the same time, I am tired of being alone and against my better judgement, I tell him my last name.

"Mikah." I whisper. Recognition of that name flashes across his face.

"Why are you saying that name?" He asks.

"Because that is my last name. Terryn Mikah was my father." His mouth drops in shock.

"Terryn… He… He was your father?" He asks in disbelief.

"Yes." I say flatly.

"No one ever found out what happened to him. I was in Discovery when he vanished. The enforcers were all pretty upset about it, and launched their own investigations. They all came to dead ends though. Your father was a legend amongst us." He said in admiration.

"I know what happened to him. I know why he disappeared, and I know who was behind it." I say as the anger I felt is slowly taking place of the hurt. London's eyebrows furrow together in confusion. He walks over to my bed and sits, motioning for me to follow suit, sitting next to him.

"What is going on? Does this have anything to do with why you and Melanie have been so buddy-buddy and so secretive lately? That's why you've been acting so strange the last few days?" He asks as he takes hold of my hand.

"You could say that." I say, and before I could stop myself from telling him, it all comes out. "What I am about to tell you, you cannot act on. You cannot do a thing about it until I graduate and I can move freely about the compound. Promise me. If you do, it could kill all of us." I plead. London embraces me in a hug, and as he pulls back from it, he looks me in the eyes and tells me that he promises. So I tell him. I tell him about my father, and why he disappeared. I tell him how the council and Jaila really operate. I tell him what Melanie has told me, and how Jaila has threatened me. As I tell him all of this, I see the reactions on his face go from shock, anger, horror, and finally to disgust.

"I promised you that I wouldn't act on this information right now, but I also promise you that when the time is right, I will be right there with you to take that bitch Jaila and that council down. How could something like this go on without anyone noticing, and for how long?" He asks, shocked.

"Because people look the other way or they're taken care of before they can say anything." I answer, my voice dripping with disdain. I see my father's face flash across my mind as I say the last part. She will get her's. Father, one day they all will.

"I just can't believe it. I can't believe that you kept this to yourself. That had to have been difficult." He says as he strokes my hair back. I lean into his chest a little bit further, ducking my head under his chin. He wraps his free hand around my shoulder, pulling me in all of the way, molding me to his body. "I'm here for you Jun with whatever you need. I wouldn't let her lay a finger on you or anyone you care about." He says this trying to reassure me. It does little to soothe me. All it does is send panic coursing through my body as it tenses.

I get up and start to pace. As much as I want there to be an 'us', it just can't be. I must tell him that. I can't let this go on any further than it has. My father, one of the most revered Enforcers, was unable to stop Jaila. What makes London think he can? I could never forgive myself if something happened to him because of me.

"What's going on in that pretty little head of yours?" He asks, his voice compassionate. How do I tell him after all that has transpired between us? Now that I had a taste of how I could feel with him, how I opened up to him, could I *really* swear him off? My heart beats erratically at the thought of it. When I look at him, it's as if he can read my mind. He stands up, eyes wide.

"Oh no. You can't be serious?!" He says as he shakes his

head in disbelief. He attempts to walk towards me, but I step away from him as he attempts to touch me. The sting of rejection is all over his face. Again, of my doing.

"Be-?" he asks, his voice full of sorrow.

I raise my hand forcing him to stop mid-sentence. "London, I can't put you in harm's way and I can't get sidetracked. If something happened to you because of me, I could never forgive myself." I say this pleading now. I don't know who I'm trying to convince at this point; him or me.

"You can't stand there and say that you didn't feel that between us at the gym, between us now. Hell, since day fucking one if I'm being honest with myself. After a kiss like that and what you just told me, I can't go back to just being friends." He says with his voice full of determination. "And what do you think Jaila and the others will find more odd? A girl avoiding everyone, or a girl being around other people?"

"I'm not denying anything when it comes to us. I'm not. But the timing of this couldn't be worse. I can't think straight or focus when I am so close to you. That is a risk all in itself." I say this trying to convince myself of why it can't be right now, more than him. "If my father couldn't stop her or the council, if he couldn't protect us, then how will you?" I say on the verge of more tears.

"Be-"

"No London. My father's way of protecting us was leaving us when Jaila and the council couldn't be stopped by him. How could I live with myself if I got you banished, if I got you killed?" I say as tears fall freely, terrified at that very real possibility.

"There is no reason for you to burden this alone. I can take care of myself and I can help protect you. Don't toss away the chemistry we have because you feel that you must protect *everybody*. Let me share that burden with you. Let me be the person you lean on. You're seventeen and carrying all of this on your shoulders. If something happened to me, that would be on me. That would not be on you. I am an adult who made this decision to want to be with you and all that comes with it." He says as he grabs ahold of one hand, moving my head up to look him in the eye with the other. Those beautiful eyes now pleading with me. "And when is it ever the right time?"

"I don't know London. I'm terrified that if I let you in, let 'us' happen, when push comes to shove, you'll be used against me in the way that Jaila and the council used my mother and I against my father, or vice versa." London gabs ahold of my shoulders and looks me square in the eye.

"We are not your parents. Just because that happened to them, does not mean that it will happen to us. There is something real between us, and I am not willing to just toss that aside. There aren't so many of us in the compound that you can just turn away from what we have brewing between us. Some never have this, and are only together out of pure necessity. We can be careful, and you deserve to have some sort of semblance of happiness. As do I."

"What will the other students say? What will the other instructors say?" I ask as I feel my resolve crumbling, grasping for any reason.

"I don't give a shit what they say. I have no say over your grades and you're not my student. There is no way for me to influence whether you pass or fail Discovery. Besides, it's not like this hasn't happened in the past. We wouldn't be the first 'student' and 'instructor' to date."

I just stare back at him in shock.

Could we make this work?

Can I trust him to be by my side?

Is this worth the risks?

Fuck it.

I grab ahold of his face as I say, "This compound and the people who run it, have taken enough from me. I won't let them deny me you any longer." I say as I crash my lips to his. He stumbles back a little I think in shock, but he does not disappoint. His tongue pushes my lips apart, and he assaults my mouth with our teeth clashing, tongues dancing, and our breaths labored. We slowly walked backwards, unintended, as the kiss deepens until the back of my knees hit my bed. We break our kiss as his lips travel down my neck, and his hands travel up my sides. My hands travel up his back, pulling him as close as humanly possible.

He hands are everywhere. Just as he begins to lift my shirt, I become well aware of where this is headed. I push back slightly, and the look on face could melt ice. It sends chills down my spine.

"I'm not ready for that just yet, no matter how much my body wants to protest." I say breathlessly as I rest my head against his.

He closes his eyes as he weaves his fingers through my hair, breathing deeply. "I can wait for that. I am just happy to be here with you like this." He says as he places a few more soft kisses on my lips.

"We have to be careful, but I am sick of letting this compound take everything from me." I say as my hands travel up the sides of his head, and into his hair.

"I'm not going anywhere." He says as he climbs in my bed, with his hand out stretched for me. I kick off my shoes and mold my body to his. We don't say anything for the rest the night. We hold each other, caressing each other, until we fall asleep. As I drift asleep, I find myself feeling something that I haven't felt in a long time.

Safe.

Chapter Ten

I wake up before the morning alarm sounds to two strong hands wrapped tightly around me. I relish in the moment a little bit, not wanting to face the real world just yet. I didn't want to leave this room. I wish I could just stay in here with him, in our little bubble.

I look up at London, and he looks so peaceful as he sleeps. As much as I hated that I'd have to wake him up before the alarm goes off, I knew that I had to. If Hazel walked in and saw me sleeping in bed with a man (not just any guy either, an instructor), she would freak out. I would never hear the end of it. All kinds of scenarios would run through her head. She would never believe that all we did was make-out and cuddle.

As I hold onto him a little tighter, I think back to last night...

What a night...

As right as him and I feel, I can't help but wonder if I did the right thing. London was right. After that kiss in the gym, there was no going back to being friends. I let it happen. I opened that door, and there was no closing it now. I couldn't deny our chemistry any more than he could. It's so strange, powerful, and scary. I'd never felt this with anyone before. Honestly? It terrifies me a little. I know I am going to catch hell from Melanie once she catches wind of it. This was not something I was looking forward to at all.

I gently bring my fingers up his arm, tracing what I could see of his tattoos. I couldn't make any of them out at the angle I was laying, or with the poor light. I was looking forward to seeing those. I traced all the way to his chest (it was solid...), lightly sweeping the tips of my fingers across his cheekbones, and his lips.

His lips...

I close my eyes, and gently give them a kiss. Before I can pull away, I feel London's arms around me tighten as his lips part, inviting me in. This kiss is different than the ones from last night. This one was slow, exploring, and adoring.

"Well that's one way to be woken up." London says with a huge grin on his face, "Good morning. I could get used to that..."

"Good morning." I smile back, chuckling. "I didn't want to wake you, but I thought it best that you leave before Hazel shows up with our breakfast and a thousand questions as to why I have the enforcer instructor sleeping with me in my bed." London's eyes grow wide as he lets go of his grip on me and sits up.

"Shit, I didn't even think about that, otherwise I would have gone back to my room last night. I'm sorry. I got so caught up in the moment. I wouldn't want to ruin your reputation. I don't care if they know we're dating, but if they think we are just hooking up, that would ruin you."

As soon as he lets go, I miss his arms around me almost immediately.

"Don't be. I've never slept next to anyone aside of my mother. I quite enjoyed it. Let them talk. They all think I'm nuts anyway. It's Hazel's thousand questions that I don't want to face." I can feel the blush creep into my cheeks as I confess.

"Jun, are you blushing?" He teases. I roll my eyes and punch him playfully as he chuckles. "I never have either, so, you know, I think I could get used to this." He smiles as he holds my hand. I don't believe him for a second.

"I find that quite hard to believe."

"Why do you say that?"

"You've never spent the night with another woman?" Realization crosses over his face as he finally gets what I'm saying.

"We weren't talking about sex before. We were talking of sleeping in the same bed overnight with the opposite sex. As far as sex goes, yes, I've been with two other women." He says nonchalantly.

Oh man. I wasn't a prude, but I'd never had sex. I've kissed, my hands had wandered, but I'd never had any kind of sex. I wasn't afraid of becoming pregnant. As soon as a girl gets her period in the compound, she is taken to the doctor to get an implant that prevents pregnancy until she decides she's ready to have a child. This is one of the reasons, because you can only have one child in the compound. Once you have one, you and your partner have to get procedures done, which takes away your ability to have any more children. You become sterile.

I don't know why it affected me that he wasn't a virgin, and that I was. I guess it was because if it ever did end up going there, I guess I would feel inadequate.

There is no way he couldn't see that something was bothering me, between the crimson on my face and the thousand-yard stare.

"Does it bother you that I am not a virgin?" He asks curiously.

I get up and walk over to my closet to get my clothes for today. I do that so my face can't give me away. As my back is to him, I tell him, "No, it doesn't."

If he doubts me, he doesn't say anything. I do feel two arms warp around me from behind a few moments later. London trails kisses up my neck and to my ear, as he whispers, "You're a terrible liar you know." I giggle, but don't say anything.

"Alright, like you said, let's avoid the thousand questions. I'll see you in a little bit." He says as he lets go of me. "Before I leave however..." he says, as he turns me around so that our faces are inches apart. He lowers his lips to mine again for a short, yet sweet kiss goodbye. "See you in the gym."

"I look forward to it." I say as he leaves. This is going to be trouble, and I know it. Another feeling that I haven't felt in a long time creeps up in me. Happiness. Happiness and hopefulness.

I can only hope it lasts...

A few minutes after he leaves, the bell rings. I quickly get dressed, walking over to Hazel's room to try to catch her before she leaves, making it to her door as she is opening it.

"Hey Jun, I see you're up and about. Going back to class today? How's your ankle?"

"Yeah. I'm doing much better. I was able to work-out in the gym last night, so it is time to get back. I wanted to thank you for all that you did. If you ever need anything, please ask." Hazel stops dead in her tracks.

"Who are you, and what have you done with my angry, 'everyone's out to get me', I can't have no one in my life, friend?" I shake my head smiling as I roll my eyes. "Seriously, you seem dangerously happy. This is very unlike you." She says squinting her eyes, sounding suspicious.

"Oh hush. I'm just happy to be out of that little room. Could you imagine being stuck in your room for a week just lying in bed, having to rely on everyone else to do the simplest things?"

"You have a point. I'm onto you though. I will find out eventually. Whether you tell me, or I find out on my own, I *will* know." She says matter-of-factly trying to get me to talk.

"Have fun trying to figure it out." I tease back.

Once we get to the showers, we part ways. Hazel, to fight for a shower with a curtain, and I, off to breakfast. I'd hoped to get there early so that I could ea, and hit the gym for about ten minutes or so before classes started. I wanted to do that because I knew that I'd be fighting today and I wanted to warm up, being that I was off my feet the past week.

I made my way down to the first floor, to the food hall. There were only two people here. I guess they all opted to shower this morning. Kinda makes me feel gross but I'd rather take it at night, so I don't have to fight for a shower with a curtain. To my surprise, it was Ira and Annia who were the two people. They were in line waiting for them to open for breakfast.

"Hey Annia, Ira!" I yell. They both look at me with smiles. Ira only waves. Annia however, waves me over to her.

"It's good to see you back on your feet Jun." Annia says excitedly.

I smile back, "Well, it's great to be back Annia. I was going stir crazy being held up in that room for a week."

"I can imagine." She says as the line opens for breakfast. We grab our scrambled eggs and make our way to a table.

"Ira, you're more than welcome to sit with us if you'd like." He looks at me like he is considering it for a moment before he shakes his head no, thanking me anyway. Annia and I look at each other a bit confused, but sit down nonetheless.

"Do you know anything about him Annia?"

"No, why do you ask?"

"Well, the last few days he has been bringing me dinner because Melanie was unable to. He would give my food, sit down to eat his, and we'd chat about nothing in particular. The second that I was done, he'd gather up our trays and leave. He'd do this whether he was done or not." Annia looked confused, and to be honest, so was I. He seemed so odd.

"That is strange. Is that normal behavior for someone in intelligence?'

"Not that I am aware of. I can't put my finger on it, but he seems so familiar to me. It's like I've known him forever, and at the same time not at all." Annia's looking at me like I've mutated an extra appendage. "I know it sounds strange. I just can't shake the feeling."

We spent the next few minutes eating because we both wanted to be out of there before all the other people got here. We finished up and said our goodbyes. I realized that I wouldn't have time to do anything of importance at the gym. I went to the classroom instead, secretly hoping Melanie would be there. I walked into the classroom, and sure enough she was there.

"Ah, Miss Mikah. It's good to see you up and about. I trust Ira was good?"

"Yes, he was fine. He was a bit odd though." I said. Melanie sat up with an apologetic look in her eye. I knew right then she was behind his acting strangely towards me.

"That's partly my fault. I told him not to get too close to you, and to leave as soon as you were done eating." She said apologetically. She saw my face and raised her hands, stopping me before I could ask her why. "I trust you Jun. Otherwise I wouldn't have confided in you, and you have to trust that. After what has happened, I don't trust anyone and neither should you. Think about it for a second. If Jaila offered someone a guaranteed spot in the compound to spy on someone and report back to her, you don't think someone would take her up on that offer?" She says just as the students start to come in. As they do, she stands to greet them.

"Hello students. Please take your seats. We have a few things to go over before we make our way to the gym. As you know, we only have two days left in the gym for training and sparring with the enforcers. I just wanted to let everyone know that you've done a fantastic job. Some of you weren't doing so hot in the first few weeks, but you trained hard and have surpassed my expectations. There will be no failures in this portion if you continue to train hard and put your best foot forward. That being said, these last two days are important. They will be used in the overall score, which will determine if you pass or fail this class. Does anyone have any questions before we head over there?"

No one makes a sound so Melanie takes that as a no. She instructs everyone to make their way to the gym. On the way over there, I can't help but think of what Melanie has said. She made a very good point.

Could I still trust my friends?

Would any of them turn on me?

I've only known these people about a month. Is that long

enough to be able to trust my life with someone?

I'm almost positive Hazel and Annia wouldn't spy on me. Ira is an acquaintance whom I don't know. Could he be a spy? What about Emelia? Being that I've already been threatened, and what I've learned about the compound, it's not unreasonable to think that it could happen. I decided that from now on, I'd trust no one else other than the people whom I've come to know and trust thus far.

This was going to be a long five months.

The closer we got to the gym, the faster my heart began to race. I was looking forward to seeing London, even though I knew that we couldn't show each other any attention during class hours. We had to be professional. I just hope he knew that. He seemed to have gotten it when he agreed to avoid the thousand questions with Hazel this morning. Once we reached the gym London was at the door...

Fuck...

He wasn't going to make this easy. Once he spotted me, he smiled in my direction. That didn't go unnoticed by Melanie. She gave me a quick glance, then looked away.

"Good morning Melanie." London said. "How are you this morning?" Melanie looked from him, then to me before answering him.

"I'm good, how are you? Are you ready for your enforcers to have their asses handed to them?" London folds his arms and laughs.

"Ahahahaha! That's a joke right? I know this is my first-year teaching, and I know the intelligence class has a better record than the enforcers when it comes to sparring each other. But as I stated earlier, this is MY first year and you my dear, have never been up against my teachings. After all, *I have* pinned you." He states matter of factly with such a shit eating grin. I couldn't help it. I smirked.

"Punk." I chuckle under my breath.

Melanie's lips curl up on the right side. You could see the anticipation radiating off of her, ready to prove him wrong. I glance over at the other classmates, and they seem to share her excitement. Everyone, including me, is up for a little competition.

"Ah, and you see, that will be your downfall. Decland, care to share with London here how underestimating me went the very first time you met me?"

With a big cocky grin, he responds. "Man, if you think just because you're new here and have that as an advantage, then you are sadly mistaken."

"Is that so? I guess we will have to see then won't we?" London teases.

The joy is short lived however because when I look back over at Melanie, I see that she looked nervous. This is odd because she's usually really good at keeping her emotions in check. I turn around to see why she looked so worried, and I see none other than Jaila and the two same enforcers who delivered me to Discovery walking towards us. I immediately look to her and London. They both had the same exact face.Worry. Worry written all over. What the hell is this about? Did someone sell me out? Panic begins to make my heart race the closer she gets to me.

"Juniper. Come with me." Jaila says sternly.

"Is there something wrong?" Melanie asks, moving to stand next to me. London is at my other side in an instant.

"I suggest the two of you move aside. This has nothing to do with either of you for the moment." Jaila threatens.

Melanie steps a little in front me, almost shielding me if you will. "She is my student. I have the authority and the right to know what is happening in regards to my students." Melanie states. London slips his hand into mine squeezing it gently, trying to reassure me. It does not work. If anything I fear more now, because I have more to lose. Goddammit! Why couldn't I have just trusted my gut and kept to myself?!

"You do not have authority over me, or over the council's affairs. Step. Aside." Oh. That *bitch!*

"She is not going anywhere without me." London

says,which causes both Melanie and I to look at him. Melanie sees our hands together, and a flash of disapproval moves across her face.

"Is that so London? Well, seeing as you're not her husband, mother, or father, you have zero say in anything to do with Juniper. Even if you were any of those things, you would still have no power to stop me. I highly suggest the both of you to step aside or face the consequences."

I let out a breath I hadn't known I was holding, mustering all of the courage I had left to muster. "London, Melanie, it's okay. I'll go. There is no need for all this." I say pointing between all of us.

London then takes a protective step in front of me, still holding my hand. "The hell there isn't." I let go of his hand, and turn him to face me.

"London, it's okay. I'll be alright." I say to him. I step closer and whisper, "If anything, Melanie will be able to find me. Work with her. Tell her you know what has been going on. I'll be okay, trust me."

Reluctantly he lets go of me. "I trust you." He says right before he kisses me in front of everyone.

"I'll be back before you know it." I say to him smiling poorly. He looked scared, and that is saying a lot. I give him one more quick kiss before looking over at Melanie. "Trust me Melanie." I say to her. She doesn't say anything. She just moves out of the way.

"I hope you're doing the right thing Juniper." Is the last thing I hear as I make it towards the first floor.

Once I am in the hallway, the enforcers stop just outside the entrance of Discovery, closing the doors behind them. Jaila looks at me before saying, "You should have listened to me Juniper." That was the last thing I remembered before the one enforcer knocked me out with the back of his gun. The last thing I see is Jaila's face. Her lips contorted in a psychotic grin.

Then there is nothing, only blackness.

Chapter Eleven

I slowly start to come to. As I do though, I realize everything hurts. I try to move my hands and feet to stand, but I can't. I am bound to a chair. I take a few breaths and look around. I am in the middle of a poorly lit room with a single door about twenty feet in front of me.

What the fuck?

Why am I here?

What did she find out?

My head begins to throb, and I can feel the room start to spin. So many questions and fears begin to swirl in my mind as the door opens.

Jaila.

"After our little chat Juniper, I really thought that you would have headed my warning. It seems I was wrong however. I know everything that you and your little friends know. Did you really think that you could overthrow me? The council and I? You and four people? Ahahahaha, that is a sad joke my dear." She says as she cackles. There really is something seriously wrong with her.

"I'm not afraid of you Jaila." I say with all the strength that I have left. She smiles as she places her face just a mere few inches away from mine.

"Well you should be. You see, just by even thinking about doing the things you wanted to do will cost you and your conspirators greatly." She threatens as she runs her fingers across my face. I shudder at her touch. Suddenly, panic sets in about the fate of my friends.

"Leave them alone. If you want to set an example, use me." Jaila stands up and laughs.

"It's a little too late for that now. You should have listened to me the first time. Besides, what do you think will be more productive? Using one example, or six? Maybe I'll do a public execution. The message will be loud and clear."

How the fuck did she find out?! After her little visit I didn't talk about anything outside of my room?!

"I bet you're wondering how I found out about what you know, and what your plans are. Well, let's just say not all of your friends are whom they seem to be. Did you really think after what your father did, that I wouldn't have placed someone in Discovery to watch over you? That I wouldn't have someone watching your every move?" She says as she circles me. "Everyone has secrets, or something that can be leveraged against them. There's always something that I can use to force their cooperation. One way or another, I *always* get what I want."

I am seething with anger and betrayal. I only became close to a few people, and knowing one of them did this turns my stomach just as much as the woman in front me of does.

"Who was it?" I asked, my voice laced with hate.

"Now why would I tell you that, when I have plans to use this person again? I am going to let you sit and think on what you've done. The danger you just placed on Melanie, London, your mother, and your father... You have no idea. Thanks to you, we know he is still alive. That will be rectified soon."

"My mother is innocent in all of this! Why does she have to be punished?!" I scream.

"Because your father was stupid enough to contact her. She has known since the beginning that he was alive and what his plans were. She didn't come forth with it. I wasn't sure she knew, but after hearing you this last week, I put a team together to find out the whole truth. So, if you think about it, your mother could have been saved. In a sense, it's your fault she's in the position that she's in now. Her treachery would have never been discovered if it hadn't been for your treachery.

"And now just because I feel like it, I am going to let you think about what your actions caused. Then when I feel you have suffered all that can be suffered, you will be thrown out of this compound to let the radiation have its way with you. We will drag you back in and execute you with the others, only after they watch you suffer." She says, her voice dripping with excitement.

"You won't get away with this Jaila!" I scream as her hand grips the doorknob to leave. She turns towards me with an evil grin plastered to her face.

"Awe, that's cute. You think you're the first to uncover the secret of the council? You're not the first, and you won't be the last. The only thing that is different with you, is that I gave you a warning. The others were dealt with immediately. Oh, and just some more food for thought Juniper, I am on my way to London's, your mothers, and your father's holding rooms." She says as she walks out of the room, and shuts the door.

"AHHHH! What the fuck!!!!!" How the fuck did she find out? She said, 'listening to you this past week.' The only people it could have been were Hazel, Annia, or Ira. Those are the only people that were in my room who could have planted something. Just when I let my guard down this shit happens! Damn it! I knew I shouldn't have said anything or involved anyone! I can't stop thinking about London, Melanie, my mother, or my father.

Holy fuck.

My father is back in the compound.

I never thought I would be meeting him in here. That's if I get to see him at all. Fuck this. I am not just going to lay down and die. I tug on the bindings that are holding me to the chair. I pull and tug with no luck. I can't even see what she used to tie me with, because my hands and legs were tied to the back of the chair. My legs were on fire because of this. I keep pulling and tugging in hopes that I could get the bindings loose. I had to get free and save them. They were in here because of me. I HAD to get free to take down Jaila and the council. They cannot continue to get away with what they've been getting away with!

Chapter Twelve

I don't know how long I've been in here. I've lost count how many times they've brought me food. My hair has grown a lot, so I knew it had to have been a while. After the first day, they let me out of my bindings and left me a bucket to use as a toilet.

Fucking gross.

I've damn near driven myself crazy with the what if's.

What have they done to the others?

Who gave me away?

How was I going to get out of here?

What have I done?

I was unbelievably stiff from laying on the hard, cold stone floor. The food they gave me seemed like scraps from their own meals. It probably was. The first few times it was given to me I refused it. But after days upon days of not eating, I caved in. I felt so disgusted by it. I knew that I had to eat it in order to stay alive. That's if I had any hope of getting out of here alive. I did what I could to keep myself in shape. It was the only thing they couldn't take away from me, and the only thing keeping me sane. The smell from the bucket made me puke a few times. I was lucky if they changed it once a day. I tried to stay positive, and I tried not to lose hope. I kept telling myself that I'd get out. After so long though, my resolve started to wane. How could it not?

The door opened taking me away from my thoughts. It was always one of the two enforcers who took me to Discovery. It seems as though they were on her payroll. He walked up to me with his weapon drawn, holding a tray of half eaten food.

"How long have I been in here?" I asked, expecting no answer. They never answered my questions.

"You've been in here for six months." Jaila says walking in behind him.

What?! Six months?! I knew it was long, but I never dreamed it to be six months.

"I simply must commend you Juniper. You seem to still have all of your wits about you. Most people cave within a few weeks."

I don't even try to hide my disdain for her. I can feel it all throughout my body. As if to give me a warning, the enforcer waves his weapon in front of me as a reminder not to try anything. She just smiles a cocky grin. I wanted to knock that fucking grin off her face.

It will happen soon.

"Why am I still here? Why haven't you gotten rid of me yet? What are you hoping to accomplish?"

She smirks, "The point was to break you. The point was to have you in complete despair before you were tossed into the radiation. But I guess you're ready to die then, aren't you?"

"There is a strong chance I won't."

"Oh I'm so very sorry! I forgot to tell you Juniper, the rules have changed since it was discovered that your father was still among the living. With many others looking to take me down, it has been decided that we will no longer offer anyone the mercy of *maybe* surviving the radiation." She says as she walks closer to me. "Turns out there were more people surviving the radiation, mutated or not than we thought." The closer she gets, I can see that she is covered in a red substance. It was all over her clothes and her hands. I guess she's not afraid to do her own dirty work.

Is that?

No…

But if it is, who's is it?

My heart drops at the possibility that it could belong to someone I care about. I know she can see it. She smiles like she has accomplished something great. I'm barely even able to form a sentence.

"Wh-who's blood is that?" I asked, barely able to get it out.

She looks at her clothes and hands, "Oh this? This would be the last remains of your mother." She says menacingly.

Cold.

Hearted.

Bitch.

I fall to my knees as all of the air in my body leaves me. My face contorts in pain as I begin to sob inconsolably, as I think of the last moments my mother was alive. She was murdered because of me...

Because I couldn't keep my mouth shut...

Because I didn't listen to Melanie.

Because against my better judgement, I trusted people and made friends.

Because against my better judgement, I confided in people...

"Why?!" I scream as a sob racks my body. Jaila laughs. She is loving every second of this. Jaila loves seeing the pain she's caused. She's a fucking psychopath!

"I already told you why she was taken. You can blame yourself for her mur-."

I don't even let her finish the sentence. I lunge at her, knocking her backwards.

"YOU FUCKING CUNT! I WILL KILL YOU!" I shout. I'm able to get in a few shots in before I feel the enforcer yank me back, tossing me to the ground. Jaila gets up and dusts herself off, looking a bit frazzled. Good, that fucking cunt deserves it. The enforcer picks me up by my neck and holds me in place in front of her.

She shows me her right knuckles which are covered in blood. "This was the last thing she felt before he put a bullet in her head." She says to me as she points at the enforcer who is holding me. I try to struggle free as hot tears escape my eyes, trickling down my face. I have never felt pure hatred and anger like I do now. I could feel it pulsing through my body. The enforcer pulls me closer, holding me still.

"Give me your weapon *now*. I want to do this one myself." Jaila seethes. The enforcer hands over his weapon without hesitation. She takes it, immediately smashing the back of it across my face. My neck jerks to the left as I feel a searing pain across my cheek that ripples down my neck. I taste iron almost instantly. I pool the blood in my mouth, waiting for an opportune time to spit it right in her face.

"Oh! That felt good!" she shouts. As she begins to laugh, I take my moment to spit my blood right in her mouth. Watching her gag is worth the punch that follows.

"You think you're swift don't you? This has gone on long enough. Enforcer, bring her to her knees." She commands.

For the first time in my life I had nothing to say. All I can think about is my mother. I wonder if this is how she felt during her last moments... A sob escapes me at the thought.

My poor mother...

In this moment I can't help but think of London. We could have been great. He was right. There was something special about us. It was an unexplainable pull that neither one of us could fight. I was only trying to prevent what is happening now. In the same respect, if I had stuck to what I said I was going to do in the first place, he wouldn't be here facing death for wanting to be with me.

If he wasn't dead already that is...

I'm so sorry London...

I open my eyes as more tears escape me, to see the barrel of the gun pointing just inches from my head. I close my eyes and I can see them all. My dad and mom happy with me, London and Melanie smiling at me...

I'm going to miss them.

"Not so fearless now, are you? It's funny how that works

isn't enforcer? You *really* get to see who is as tough as they seem to be when certain death is upon them. What a coward."

All of my senses are heightened. I can hear the droplets of water hitting the floor from the rock above, and feel the little bit of air circulating around the room. I can feel each droplet of sweat rolling down my body. I can hear Jaila's finger glide over the trigger when I hear gunshots. It wasn't from Jaila though. I open my eyes to see who was shooting, but I can't see anyone as I'm shoved into the wall. I hit it pretty hard, but I am able to get my senses in order when I hear him.

"Juniper! Run to me!" It was London! Oh thank god! He wasn't killed! I am filled with renewed hope as I stand up to run (dodging a barrage of bullets in the process) to the sound of his voice. Once I reach him he pulls me out of the room, jamming the door closed, locking Jaila and the enforcer inside.

"You better run far and fast, because once I catch you, you're both *dead!*" Jaila screams from the other side of the door.

Once the door is secure, London looks me over. He sucks in a quick breath when he sees their handy work on my face and body. His face is turning red with anger. I can only imagine what he sees. He places a gentle hand on my face, examining me.

"Are you okay? Can you run?" He asks.

"I can run."

"Okay, follow me. That door is not going to hold much longer, and I need to get your mother yet. Melanie has a safe house for us to hide in until we can safely get outside." At the mention of my mother, more tears flow. London's brows furrow together in confusion.

"She-she's...she's been murdered by Jaila..." I barely get out. London's mouth drops a little in shock.

"Are you sure she killed her?" He asks, disbelieving.

"She showed me the blood on her hands, and told me that's all that was left of her." I all but sob. London pulls me into a hug, kissing the top of my head. We stay there for brief moment as the tears run freely.

"I'm sorry Jun and I hate to do this, but we have to go." I

wipe the tears from my eyes and agree. If we stood any chance of getting out of here, we needed to move and move fast. I follow him through a maze of tunnels that I have never seen before. We get about ten minutes into the run and I nearly fall over from exhaustion. I stop abruptly, which causes London to stop.

"Jun, are you okay?" London asks, full of concern.

"I ca- I can't run anymore." I get out through heavy breaths.

"Alright, I'll carry you. We can't stop now. We're close to the hideout. Jaila has more than likely escaped by now and is already looking for us.

I don't even protest. He picks me up with ease and begins to run. I rest my head along his collarbone and hold onto him tight, afraid that this is a dream that I might wake up from. Being in his arms, I felt safe. I felt protected.

I'm not sure if it was the rocking or the fact that I was exhausted, but within a few minutes of being in his arms I passed out. The last thing that I remember was looking up at London. This was before the darkness took me.

Chapter Thirteen

"Oh god London, is she okay?" I faintly hear a woman ask. Is that Melanie?

"I really don't know. She looks really malnourished... and...she's in pretty bad shape." He says. He sounds so upset. I can't say that I would be any better off if I had found him the same way that he found me.

I can feel London put me down onto something soft and I can hear someone approaching me. Why the hell can't I open my eyes? My body feels like a boulder landed on me and I can barely move.

"Jesus London, what happened to her?" Yep, that's definitely Melanie. "She is covered in bruises and her face is swollen." She says, her voice full with worry.

I am finally able to open my eyes, and I try to speak. I get nothing more than a squeak out which catches their attention. London turns as he faces me. His face is taught with worry, shock, and relief.

"Juniper, you're awake!" He shouts.

"Quiet down London! Let's try and not give away our location because you can't control yourself." Melanie scolds as she walks up behind him.

I take a few deep breaths while my eyes adjust to the light.

"Wh-where are we?" I ask. Why the hell does my voice sound so fragile?

"We're safe. Do you remember your escape?" London asks, as he caresses my face gently. As he says that, the events that led up to it now flash before me. Oh dear god, my mother! I think back to what Jaila said and showed me before London saved me. I begin to cry inconsolably.

London holds me as the tears fall freely. After a few minutes, I regain control of my emotions. "We need to figure out if what Jaila said was true...If she really did murder my mother. We need to find the person who sold me out as well."

"Agreed." Both London and Melanie say.

"I wonder who it could have been?" Melanie thinks aloud. "We were so careful."

"Well there are only three people it could have been. Annia, Hazel, or Ira." I say. The both of them look at me curiously. "I say that because it was only those three that were ever alone with me, or that I was close with."

"I don't think that it could have been Hazel or Annia" I wonder aloud.

"Why do you say that?" London asks.

"Because they were never alone with me while I was not aware. The only person that was, was Ira."

"I'm not sure it was him. I had him thoroughly checked out before I let him bring food to you when you were injured." Melanie states.

"I understand that, but there was one time that I had fallen asleep for maybe about ten minutes while he was in my room, after he brought me some food. If he was searching for anything, it would have been enough time to find something or plant something. All Jaila would've had to do is threaten him with being tossed out if he didn't comply with her wishes. That would be enough for anyone to do as she asked." I say.

London and Melanie look at me with matching curious, slightly troubled looks.

"What?"

"How come you never told us this before?" Melanie asks, beating London to it.

"Because I didn't think too much of it at the time and there was nothing damning in my room. They only thing that I took with me from my apartment was a family photo. Any note you gave me was destroyed as soon as I was done reading, as per your request." I say to her.

"That's definitely long enough to plant a listening device." London says as he looks from me up to Melanie. She just sat there for a moment, letting it all sink in.

"You're sure that no one else could have planted it?" She asks.

"I'm almost certain. He was the only one who could have had the time to plant it that I am aware of. Unless someone broke in while I wasn't in there to plant something..."

"Impossible. I am in intelligence, and with whom you are, I had your room watched when you were not in your room. You know, just in case someone got the idea to do just that." She says. "We need to make sure before we jump to any conclusions. I will investigate this further and look into Juniper's mother. London, keep an eye on her. Your only priority is to keep her safe and get her well. If I don't come back in three days time, you know what you have to do."

"What are you talking about? Do what?" I ask. Melanie looks at me once before she turns and leaves. What the fuck was that? What the hell are they talking about?

Once she leaves, London closes his eyes in relief as he takes a deep breath in and out. I hate that I've caused him this grief. He turns to me, taking my hands into his, kissing each of my knuckles. "Dear god Juniper, I'd thought I'd never see you again." My heart breaks at his words. I knew that feeling all too well. "Five months. Five months had passed before we heard anything on you. It took another month of planning to get you out..." A single tear escapes his left eye as he speaks. "Finding you the way that I did... It took all of my strength not to murder those pieces of shit where they stood...

"I'd prepared myself for the worst. If I'd found you dead, I fully planned on killing everyone in there. Once I saw you on your knees with a gun to your head, I saw red. I knew that I had to get you out as soon as possible; Jaila and her minions be damned." He gently brought his lips to mine for a soft, gentle kiss. When his eyes opened, I saw a pair of sad, worn, tortured baby blues staring deeply into my eyes. I gently cradle his face into my hands as a few stray tears escape my eyes, rolling down my cheeks.

"I'm sorry to keep hurting you. Thank you for not giving up on me, for not giving up on us."

"I could never give up on you, not ever." He says as he places his hands over mine. "You took a hold on my heart the very first time I saw you, and the hold grew firmer the more I got to know you as time went on. The moment I knew I had you, I was in disbelief. When you kissed me the way you did in the gym... I just... I thought to myself, holy shit it's actually happening! She wants me the way I've wanted her for so long. Don't fuck it up douchebag. She's not like the others, she's special. She's one of a kind. My heart shattered when you jumped up and ran from me like I did something wrong. I was on the verge of tears, but utter shock froze me in place. Seeing you run away from me like that actually made me fear that I'd never see you again. Going through what you just did now, that realization could have happened so easily had I not chased you down and made you see reason-no, let me finish love, please." He says as I try to say to say something.

"I waited till lunch for you to come back. When you didn't, I found Melanie. When she said that she hadn't seen you, panic shook us to the core. I have never felt such loss, and crippling heartbreak ever before in my life. We feared the worst knowing what Jaila is capable of. The one thing we couldn't find no matter how hard we searched, we couldn't find any evidence of your death or expulsion. We held onto hope. Your friends would vanish only to come back different people. They refused to talk to anyone and kept to themselves. Once your mother vanished and never came back, we followed that trail. That trail eventually led to finding the room we thought you to be in."

"How were my friends the last time you saw them? How did Jaila not get a hold of you and Melanie?"

"The night you didn't return, Melanie and I went into hiding. She had this safe house put aside a long time ago, as a just in case. This is her family's original fall-out shelter from just before the surface above went nuclear. Most of the locations of the original shelters have been forgotten or salvaged to make new, updated homes. They've also been used to create the new technologies and hardware which have allowed us to be underground for as long as we've been. As far as your friends go, what we know of them has been through other people who've been keeping an eye on things for Melanie and I. Only one of us would leave at a time. That kept things safest. If one of us got caught, then there would still be one of us able to look for you."

I was in a state of disbelief as he was talking. Hearing what everyone has gone through, and hearing what had happened because of my self-righteous attitude... Why couldn't I just leave everything be? Why couldn't I just stick to the plan I had going into Discovery and just stayed to myself? If I had done that, neither of these two things would have come to pass. Everyone would be alive and well. I just *had* to come into their lives and fuck it all up.

"Hey, don't you dare do that." London says as he places his hand under my chin, forcing me to look at him. I just look at him unable to speak. I try to turn my head away because I can't even bare to look at him, not after everything that I caused. He holds his hand firmly in place though, making it impossible.

"Don't you dare. This type of shit has been going on long before us. You didn't cause something to happen that wouldn't have happened eventually. What has happened is not your fault. Stop blaming yourself."

I yank my chin away and roll over as best as I could. I couldn't even look at him right now. "Please, I just need sometime to myself right now. So much has happened, I need some time to process it all." I didn't have to see his face to know I hurt his feelings. I felt a kiss on my head, then the cushions move from his departure.

Chapter Fourteen

I wake up to hear the door slide open. It makes this horrible screeching sound as it slides across the rock floor. The enforcer walks in, gun firmly in his hand with Jaila right on his heels. I'm not sure how long I've been in this hole. I've lost count of the number of times that I've fallen asleep in this chair. The floor was far too cold and damp to sleep on. I could feel Jaila's eyes on me before I see her walk from behind the enforcer.

"I see that you've made yourself at home in that chair. I could see that you get a mattress and maybe a blanket, if you would just tell me who your accomplices are..." Jaila says to me, trying to bribe me. It will never work. I'd never turn on my friends. Her words dawn on me then. She doesn't know everything as she claimed. Unable to control the smile that spread across my face, I look directly at her.

"Oh you silly girl, what could you possibly have to smile about?"

"Nothing much. It's just that you clearly don't know everything if you're in here willing to ease my suffering *if*, I give you information." I say as tauntingly as I could. But, as soon as I get the last word out, my smile vanishes. In two strides she is over to me in an instant, with her hand tightly wrapped around my neck. She picks me up and slams me into the rock behind me, effectively knocking whatever breath was still inside of me out. My whole body jerks back in response. I'm far too weak to fight her off, but my pride won't let me go without a fight. She slaps away my feeble attempts to free myself of her grip. Her own sick grin spreads across her face as she watches me struggle.

"Come forth enforcer. Hold her still from behind." With a brief nod of the head and 'mam', he had me secure in seconds. She released her hold just a little, enough for me to breathe. She brings her face directly in front of mine as she speaks.

"I may not know whom all is involved, but I know what you wanted to do. I know you know the secret of this compound. If I wanted to, I could just kidnap and kill anyone you became on a first name basis with, just to be sure to cover all the tracks. I could snatch them up one by one, or maybe falsify evidence that proves them guilty of something that warrants them being thrown out, or even just out right executed. That would be a lesson not forgotten anytime soon. I could start with Londo-."

I saw red as adrenaline filled my body in seconds. By a miracle I was able to free myself and put my hands around her neck. I was pulled off in a second by the enforcer and slammed against the wall, his hand firmly holding me against it. I looked up at Jaila. She was smiling?! Dear god... She really is a psychopath.

"That would get you to talk wouldn't it? If I found him and brought him in? If I got a chair and tied him right there against that wall? Only maybe I would have chains installed, and chain him so he couldn't sit? Hmm, yes... I think that is what we will have to do enforcer. Double our efforts in finding him and Melanie. I will see to the chains being installed." She said all this so calmly, so deep in thought that it made my skin crawl.

"You sick bitch! I will never, EVER, tell you a fucking thing!" I screamed. In a few strides she was next to me again.

"You know, I'm really getting tired of this mouth of yours. How about we wash it out? Will that clean up your vocabulary choices?" She seethed as she grabbed my face, with little specs of her spit hitting it. "Bring me some soap enforcer. I'm going to scrub her mouth clean."

I tried to pull away, but I was too weak. She only laughed at my attempts. It only took the enforcer a few minutes to gather what was needed. It was disturbingly amazing how he did everything that she asked. He never asks questions, never flinches, and never says no. How could someone just follow someone else so blindly? How could someone be okay with doing the things she was asking of them on a daily basis?

The enforcer brought the bucket filled with soap over to Jaila. A smile of great anticipation on her face caused my stomach to drop. Psychopath...

"How despicable. You are the *biggest* piece of shit!" I spat at her. My arms and legs were straining against her hold. Despite how I tried to keep myself in shape, it was damned hard to do off of scraps. She had me pinned to the wall using just her arm, and I was too weak to escape.

"Hold her down enforcer. I wish to enjoy this a little. I want to see her suffer." My heart was pounding in my chest the closer he got to me. The more I struggled to free myself, the more she laughed. "You're fucking psych-!" I felt the cracking of the enforcers knuckles across my cheek-bone as they collided with my face. The force of that hit loosened the grip Jaila had, and I went sailing to the floor. The enforcer went behind me and held me in place. I attempted to turn my head so that I could face him, but it was impossible.

"She must have some serious dirt on you for you to help her in this madness. I can't imagine *anyone* who would get off on thi-ahh!" He yanked my hair, causing my head to snap back and his mouth to be directly next to my ear.

"Did it ever occur to you that I like it?" That was the first time that I ever heard him speak. His voice was sinister, so deep. It sent shivers down my spine. Jesus, what the hell did I get myself involved in? What the fuck did I get my friends involved in?! Is the entire council this sadistic?! The fear I felt just then was different then any fear I felt before. I had assumed she was using something against this enforcer for him to able to do these cruel acts... I never imagined that he was here on his own free will... I closed my eyes and choked back my fear as he flung my head forward.

What he said next was absolutely terrifying. "I'm going to enjoy this one more so than the others... You see I had a thing for your mom. She continued to reject me, and ended up marrying your father. She knew that I was the better man and yet, she chose the tool. If I can't have her, well her daughter would the next best thing. I get a taste of what it would've been like had she chose me, and I get to make a dishonest woman of his precious baby girl." He tied my arms behind my back and held onto me from behind. My struggle was feeble, and all it seemed to do was make them happy. They liked to watch their victims struggle. I swear he could smell the fear on me. My insides were all over the place. I couldn't believe what was happening... Oh god, oh god, oh god, not like this. London's face briefly flashed before my eyes. I'm so sorry I failed all of you...

"Now now, you'll get your due enforcer, in due time. It is my turn now." She said so seductively. There was no point in hiding my fear anymore. It was written all over my body. They seemed to like that, watching me struggle, watching me suffer. She took a few shots at me before she preceded to scrub my mouth out with soap. She landed a few good ones. She didn't let me rinse my mouth out with water. She said she wanted me to remember the feeling when I decide to speak trashy, and to think better of it. She hit me so hard before she left that I saw actual stars before I lost consciousness, falling the rest of the way to floor.

On my way down I see the enforcer come my way, yelling, "Juniper!" What the? As I hit the floor, my body shakes.

"Juniper?! Wake up Juniper. You're having a bad dream." London pleads as he gently shakes me.

"What?" My voice was thick with sleep. Then it hits me that I was reliving a portion of my imprisonment in my dreams. I rub my eyes, wincing, forgetting the condition I'm in. Fuuuck. She will forever haunt me...

"You were whimpering at first, then I heard crying, then I heard screaming. You kept saying that 'you would never give us up. Not for anything.' Then I heard you plead..." I could hear the longing in his voice. He wanted me to tell him about it... He wanted me to tell him about my time with Jaila... I wanted to. I really did. I just didn't know if I ever could. "I woke you up because I couldn't stand to listen to you in so much agony anymore. It sounded like you were reliving it."

I looked at him and the way he was looking at me, so concerned and so full of love, it almost came out right then. I stopped myself when I looked down at the floor and saw a small makeshift bed. Even after the way I treated him, he still had to make sure I was okay. He followed my gaze and smiled sheepishly at me. "When I came to check on you, I saw that you had fallen asleep... I couldn't help myself... I'd been away from you for so long and my last memory of you was seeing that gun pressed to your head. It's all pretty much been a blur from then, up until now. I'm still in shock that you're actually here if I'm being honest with myself. I really couldn't stand to be away from you any longer. I made the bed next to you, and told myself 'to hell with it if she gets angry.'"

I was in awe. There he was, this man that's been in my head all these months. The one. Even after all this time has passed, he never gave up on me. He never gave up on us. I couldn't stop myself, nor did I want to. Jaila had taken so much from me. So much... But she failed at taking London away from me, and I'd be damned if I let what's happened do that for me.

At first he was hesitant, unsure if he should. But desire soon took over, and he met my kiss with just as much force, if not more. It was gentle at first, purposely slow. It was slow. Not just to savor it, but to make sure that it wouldn't hurt given my current state. It didn't. Slowly the kiss intensified, his hands roaming my face and my body. Every time we'd part for air, he'd whisper how he'd missed me, how he needed me and how he'd never again let me out of his sight. Against my thoughts, I believed him. In that moment I knew he'd meant every word.

Instead of fighting my inner self on how this can't be happening now, that it's a bad idea, I shut her up. I went with it. All my life I tried to be what I should. I tried to live up to what was expected of me, tried doing the right thing, and I tried to control my urges. Where the fuck did that get me? It got me kidnapped, possibly caused my mother's death, and separated me from the only man who chased after me when I ran from him. The only man who stood by me. The only man to rescue me from certain death. Nope. This time, the girl inside me died, and the woman inside rose to take what I longed for so long, what I thought I didn't need, what I thought I could no longer have. And guess what? Every caress, every kiss, every nibble, the little bit of pain, was worth it. I was London's and he was mine.

I woke up and prayed that what just happened, actually happened and wasn't just another dream. That thought was confirmed when I found myself eye level with London's nipple. We were naked. I half sprawled on his muscular body, both of his arms wrapped securely, and protectively around me. The thought briefly passed that this was a stupid idea, but I ignored it. I in no way regret what happened last night. We both needed it, and it only brought us closer. I would never leave this man's side again.

Emboldened by my actions last night, coupled with this unwavering need to have him again, I bring my tongue to his nipple and gently massage it with my tongue, occasionally sucking on it. His arms tighten around me as I hear him moan my name. This emboldens me even more, and I gently caress my hand over his bare chest down his abs to his inner thigh. Suddenly, I feel his arms pull me from his chest to his mouth, and I'm welcomed with a passionate kiss. His hands began traveling up through my hair, pulling me even closer to him. They make their way down my back to my ass, with a not so gentle squeeze. I slide my body over him, and I can feel every inch of him. *Every* inch. Our bodies begin to take over where our minds have stopped. Our hips move in tune, pressing up against each other.

Soon he rolls us over, and places my legs on either side of him. I gently push him towards me with my legs, eager to have him again, needing him. It's a little alarming in that moment when I realized that yes, I did need him. He pulls back a little bit though. He looks up at me so full of want and need, that I nearly explode. He looks to be in ecstasy, and as he bites that damned lip, he whispers "Not just yet. Last night happened so fast and so unexpectedly, that I wasn't able to treat you right." He lowers his lips to mine and kisses me, freely caressing every inch of my body. His lips move from my lips and they gently dance over my neck to my ear. *Dear god*, the sensations running through me are like nothing that I've ever felt before. With every caress and every kiss, chills run rampant over my body. I have no more control of my body's actions. Right now, it has a mind of its own.

His kisses and gentle nibbles make their way down to my breasts. My body is curling up into his, as he pays my taught nipple the same treatment I paid his not long ago. His hot breath on my body, and his warm tongue on my burning skin is almost too much to bare. I never thought it was like this. I never thought it could be this way. The emotions and the intimacy of it all. Laying there completely exposed and completely trusting the person you're with to be there with you in that moment, and nowhere else. To feel the things you feel, to be together as one being. And, to be able to bring him to this state of want, of hunger, of need. To feel his taught muscles, to be able to feel him and pull him to me, to surrender completely to each other's needs...

I'm unable to speak coherently as my head flies to the pillows, my body moving in all directions. I feel two strong hands hold my hips firmly in place and he continues his ministrations between my legs as his lips nibble, and kiss the inside of my thighs. Soon though, his hands stop and his face disappears. His hands hold my ass firmly down, and my vision goes white. Every muscle in my body is taught. The breath is literally stuck in my throat as my toes curl so much, they about fall off. His face emerges smiling *brilliantly*, as he watches my body tremble from head to toe. He kisses and feels his way back up to my lips, kissing me deeply as he holds himself above me.

"Please tell me this is real Jun, that I'm not going to wake from this alone in my room still trying to find you with Melanie." He whispers in between kisses. "I could not bare it. Having you completely and wholly, and then waking up to nothing would absolutely destroy me." He whispers in my ear. I can only echo those same words back to him. I wrap my legs around his waist, adjusting my hips, pulling him into me. He gasps at the sudden feeling.

"I am real. You are real, and this is real. I'm not going anywhere." With those last coherent words, our bodies take over and all rational thought is out in the dirt.

The smell of eggs wakes me, causing my stomach to grumble so hard that it hurts. Instinctively, my hand moved to the side of me feeling for London. The then realization hit me. He was making food! I sat up slowly and stretched a little to test out the damage I caused engaging in the activities that I did the night before. I knew I was going to pay for it, but I just didn't care anymore. I winced as pain traveled the length of my body. Yup. Definitely hurting.

I sat up, proceeded to go and look for my clothes, and was baffled. They had vanished... The smell of the eggs was getting closer. I was fighting the urge to run after him and steal them. Living off of scraps the last few months really left a lot to be desired. I heard him coming closer to the room and irrationally went and hid my naked body under the blankets we shared just hours ago; sleeping naked next to each other, amongst other things... Get a grip Juniper, he's already seen it. Still, my irrational side wins and I slide into the bed and pull the covers up to my armpits, effectively covering everything. Mere moments later, London comes walking in carrying two large plates of scrambled eggs; in nothing but his underwear... He catches me staring, and smirks; what an ass. I can't stop the smile that spreads across my face at the site of it though.

He walks over to the other side of the bed, placing a plate

in front of me. I don't even wait for him to have the plate fully down before I begin to devour the eggs. I must have eaten that entire plate in three seconds flat. I look up at London kind of embarrassed that my hunger took over like that, and his eyes are as wide as the realization that crosses his features. He places his plate down in front of me, still kind of in shock.

"Jesus Jun... I knew you'd have been fed abysmally, but I never.. Please eat mine. You should've eaten sooner. Try not to eat this plate so fast though, otherwise you will get sick. After you're done eating, we need to assess where you're at, and begin work on getting your strength back."

I finished a little slower this time. The feeling of being full from eating enough food is enough for me to start crying hysterically. London moves over and holds me tight. I couldn't believe how close I came to losing it all. I was close to never seeing anyone again, never being able to be this close with London. All of these thoughts just kept replaying over and over again, but they soon fade. All I can hear is London whispering over and over, "It's okay, I'm here now. I won't let anyone hurt you. I won't let anyone take you." We stayed like that for a moment. I cried, and he held me while I did.

Flashbacks of the horror I'd endured these last few months, the thought that maybe my mother really is dead... All these new, old, and raw emotions were taking their toll. I held on to him. I held on so tight for fear of waking up, this being all a dream. Some sick twisted illusion of Jaila's to break me. It couldn't be so real though if it were fake, could it? I can feel his arms around me, protecting me. I can feel every inch of him holding me close. He too, is afraid he might wake up and this all might be just a dream. I hold him a little tighter before I pull myself together. I wanted to sear these moments into my brain, just in case.

I try to pull away, but he holds me in place. "Just a few more minutes." He whispers into my ear. He squeezes me one final time before he lets go.

"Thank you for breakfast." suddenly shy with how I ate,

"It was delicious." He smiles warmly at me.

"You're more than welcome. I can see you were given the bare minimum to keep you alive.. I should have offered to feed you sooner. I'm so sorry."

"Don't be sorry. I doubt I could have eaten. Besides, I needed to work up an appetite first." I tease him as I nibble on his arm. His face turns a few shades of red as he smiles. Truth be told, I'm quite shocked with the way I've been so bold about sex. I surely don't feel ashamed. I did what I did because I have genuine feelings for this man. I wanted to know all of him, and my time spent with Jaila reminded me how quick I could die. I didn't want that to happen and never know him completely. I can hear my mother telling me how I should have waited. Honestly though? We both cared deeply for each other, and in this life nothing is guaranteed. Jaila can never take what we just shared away from us. Not now. Not ever.

I can feel someone's eyes on me, and know its London. I smile playfully at him, lord knows when we will have time like this again. "Like what you see?" I ask teasing him, lifting the sheet, showing nearly all of my bare legs. A wicked grin comes over his features as he uses his hands to slowly move up my thighs, kissing them along the way.

"Oh, I think you know I do. I've liked what I've seen since I first met you. From your thick legs, your perfectly round ass, your toned body, to your soft breasts, to your very inviting neckline, your perfect cheekbones, to your stunningly green eyes."

Jesus! He felt and kissed his way up my body as he said those words, revealing more and more of my naked body to him as he pulled away the sheet on his way up. He stopped mere inches from my face, allowing for his hands to caress it. "It's more than just your physical appearance." He chuckled at my eye roll. "Of course that's what first caught my attention. I am a man. But it's who you are, and how you carry yourself that has kept me interested."

"Or ya know, it could be that I made you work for it." I say chuckling. He laughs back rolling his eyes this time.

I love this. Us bring here with no walls around us. We're free to be young and happy. I can hear my sorrows still in the back of mind. I have to constantly fight to keep that at bay. I will enjoy these moments with London. Not only that, I need to have a clear mind for what we are about to endure. I simply have no time to grieve or feel sorry for myself.

Chapter Fifteen

"Do you think that I won't kill you? Is that why you're not cooperating? Are you hoping for that so your imprisonment will be over? Have you learned nothing? I get too much enjoyment from torturing you to simply kill you. I will drag this on for as long as I want. Could be days, could be months. Hell, I could drag this out for *years* if I so choose."

Jaila and her Enforcer have been taking turns with torturing me. I got whatever felt good to them that day. They have been trying for a few days now to get me to talk. *Fat chance.* Suddenly my face flies right, taking full force from the butt of the gun the enforcer was holding. Instantly, my mouth was full of iron. I could feel it pool in my mouth. The grin on Jaila's face grew wider.

"That's enough for now. Let her sit for a few days. Let's see how she feels after not eating, in, let's say four days? Bring me the chair, and the chains. We're gonna lock her in the chair, and for the love of radiation, make sure you chain the chair to floor this time too enforcer. We do not want a repeat of last time."

"Mam'.'"

"You can do as you wish with me, but I will never give you what you want." I said with as much conviction as I could, spitting out the blood still pooling in mouth.

I look up from the floor because I can hear her walking towards me. She kneels down right next to me and whispers with a sickening edge to her voice, "You, my dear, have no idea what I am capable of. I will get you to crack, and when I do, that will be the time that I will hurt you the most.....Juniper, Juniper!"

What the fuck?

"Juniper! Juniper!!"

Jaila grabs me and throws me to the floor. On my way down, my eyes pop open and my heart is pounding. I can feel the cold sweat trickling down my body. I blink my eyes a few times to see a very concerned London.

"Juniper, wake up!" He shouts as he shakes me.

"London stop. I'm awake!" I place my hands over his arms and he immediately stops shaking me, taking a deep breath.

"You scared the shit out of me." He said with a blank stare.

Holy fuck. I was dreaming of what happened to me again. I close my eyes and exhale loudly. This is never gonna stop. She was right.. No matter what, she will always haunt me. She fucking wins...

"Hey! Snap out of it! It was only a nightmare." London says, his voice cracks a little.

"I can never escape her, she'll have a hold on me one way or another..." It feels like I am having an out of body experience. I can hear my voice, sounding far away as the new realization then hits me... Jesus Christ, I will never be free of her! She's even penetrated my dreams. Nowhere's safe! No one's safe! Holy fuck, holy fuck, holy fuck, holy fuck! I can feel my heart rapidly beat harder, being able to feel each bead of sweat on my face. I can feel the bed shaking underneath me, so I look down and see that my hands are shaking uncontrollably. My breath is catching in my throat, and I'm beginning to panic. I can faintly hear London, and he's freaking out. I blink my eyes a few times, trying to calm my nerves. It's not working. No, no, no, no, no! GET THE FUCK OUTTA MY HEAD!!!!!!! "AHHHHHHH!"

"London! What the? What the hell is going on here?!"

"Melanie! Thank god you're here! I woke her up from a

nightmare. She was screaming and crying in her sleep. Then all of a sudden it sounded like she was choking and couldn't breathe. I snapped her out of it and woke her up. But then she started sweating profusely, shouting and shaking! I don't know what's wrong with her! Right before this happened she said that she could never escape her, and that she'd have a hold on her one way or the other."

"Okay. Please get back away from her, let me next to her."

"No, tell me what to do. I want to help."

"London I swear to god if you don't move I'm going to move you myself. MOVE. Thanks. Juniper can you hear me?"

I could hear them the whole time though, they sounded far away. From sheer panic, I began to mumble. "Melanie, London, please make her go away. Make her go away! She'll never stop!" I knew I was in hysterics now, but I just couldn't shake this fear. It was crippling. Melanie grabbed each of my shoulders and held me firm.

"Juniper listen to me. You are going through a panic attack. You need to try to calm down, and control your breathing. London and I are right here. We're here Juniper. She didn't get you or us. You're safe right now. That's it, deep breath in, deep breath out, in through your nose, and out of your mouth. Don't let them win, don't show them any weakness."

Slowly but surely, what Melanie tells me to do begins to work. My arms stop shaking and I am able to control my breathing.

"That's it, control your breathing. Juniper. I know you don't want to talk about what happened, and if you don't want to talk to me about what happened, that's fine. You should talk to someone though. If you don't, this is going to continue to happen."

I closed my eyes and rolled my head back against the pillows. I knew that she was right. "Guys, I really can't bring myself to get into specifics right now. By looking at me, you know I've been tortured. I've been starved. Jaila and her enforcer got into my head. I can't stop dreaming about my time there. I just feel as though I'm never truly going to be rid of her. And the thought that my..my..my mother is *dead*. I just can't handle it..." I say as a few tears escape, rolling down my cheek.

"Fucking cunt!" I flinch as London punches the table.

"London ca-." Melanie says in an attempt to calm him.

"No! Fuck that bitch, and the enforcer! I wish I had gotten a better look at him so I could have identified him. I don't understand why she has to be this way! She is completely insane!"

"I honestly think it's a symptom of being trapped underground..." I say meekly. Both London and Melanie's faces snap in my direction, full of questions. "Remember your history lessons? Before the world went to war again, scientists and governments began to explore the possibility of living underground. They feared, and rightly so, that another world war now involving nuclear power could, and would wipe out the world on the surface. They began experiments to see what species could survive to sustain a pocket of humans underground. They needed to keep the human race alive until the surface became safe to inhabit again. They began inventing the technology needed to be able to live long term underground. A lot of it was groundbreaking technology; using the earth's core for most of it, tapping into the raw power and heat from it."

"Yeah, I remember. I also remember when a small group in the team decided that it wasn't right to damn the rest of the world without some knowledge to save themselves. They were able to release simple bunker designs which would last during a nuclear attack before they were caught." London finished for me. "Humans were never meant to live underground."

"Well, humans have only themselves to blame. Greed, jealousy, and straight up ignorance got us here. Do we even know what the last war was about?" I ask. Not even my mother knew what happened, and she had devoted her life to learning, to teaching.

"Only small bits and pieces of knowledge remain from that time that we know of. The people that survived and thrived in this compound only passed down what happened through word of mouth. Over time, stories were changed and embellished, so no one really knows exactly what happened. The only thing that *has* remained a constant through all of this, was that it started out with one country pointing nuclear weapons at America first. In defense, America pointed them at the opposite country. Then other countries secretly pointed them at each other. It has been forgotten who launched the first nuke, but that first one was a domino effect, with all the other countries following suit. No one knows why anybody would launch such weapons in the first place. Everyone knew that it would wipe themselves, and their enemies off the surface of the earth bringing an end to humans and ninety-nine percent of all life on Earth." Melanie said, filling us in a little more than what was taught in school.

"How selfish can people be? Why would they want to do that?" I ask.

"Just look at Jaila. She's a perfect example. Why torture and kill the last humans (to our knowledge) on earth? She knows that we're stuck here for an immeasurable amount of time, right? Who knows? Maybe she snapped and lost her mind. My parents always said that Jaila was always ambitious, but never cruel. No one knows what happened to her that turned her into the monster that she is today though." London added.

As soon as I sat up, my stomach felt like a rock. "I don't care what happened to her. That is no excuse to murder and torture people into doing your bidding to get your way. There is something mentally wrong with that woman. She was laughing and getting sick enjoyment out of torturing me..." I confess. I could see her sick grin appear as if she were standing directly in front of me. I shivered at the thought. "There is nothing remotely good about that woman. She deserves everything that comes her way." I said it with so much hatred, that my voice was dripping with it.

London scoots closer to me, placing his arms around me. "I agree with you one hundred percent." He says as he kisses the top of my head. "There is no excuse for her. Please believe Jun that she will get what is coming to her."

I close my eyes and breathe deeply, allowing myself the sliver of comfort in his touch; in his words. I let myself have a few more moments in that comfort, locking it in my safe space before coming back to reality. Now that my episode is taken care of, my focus goes to Melanie and if she has found out anything. I sit myself up a little, attempting to sit comfortably. "Melanie, do you have any news?"

"Nothing concrete. Jaila has locked down Discovery, and is refusing to tell anyone why. Your two friends have vanished. And Ira? The one I sent to tend to you while you were ill? He has also vanished. There is still no word on your mother though. People are asking questions of her whereabouts, as she is a teacher and held in high regard. She'll have to say something, or produce a body pretty soon."

I visibly flinch at the mention of a body, and it takes all of what's left of me not to break down and lose it. Melanie sees my reaction and immediately apologizes. "Shit, Juniper. I'm sorry. I have terrible bedside manner. Forgive me for not using my head?" She asks as she taps it.

I close my eyes and shake my head. Why would she need my forgiveness? "None needed Melanie." I raise my hands, motioning for London. I barely say his name above a whisper. Until this very moment, I hadn't realized how much I needed his support. Without missing a beat, he is sitting next to me in just a few minutes. I curl up in his embrace, needing to soak up some of his strength, needing to feel safe in his arms. That was the only place I felt safe anymore. We sit there like that gently rocking, my head tucked under his arm.

I can feel Melanie's stare, but, this time I feel no disappointment. "I knew this was going to happen sooner or later. Let me just say that I was never against you two ever getting together, it was just the timing of it all. London, I had an idea of the road that lay ahead for Juniper, and I didn't want you to get caught up in it in fear of this very scenario." She says as she waves her hands around proving her point.

I understand why she did what she did. That doesn't mean I liked her trying to replace my mother. "How many more days can we stay here? What I need is a solid day to just rest. No talking, no nothing, just sleep."

"I'm not sure, a few days maybe? We can't stay in any one place for too long."

"That's fine." I say as I untangle myself from London. He kisses the top of my head before letting me go, pulling me into a gentle hug. As he tries to stand I place my hands on his thighs, preventing him from doing so.

"Please stay. I think I would be able to actually sleep if I knew that you were next to me. At least until I actually fall asleep?" As I say it, I know how weak it sounds. I'm just tired of reliving my abduction in my dreams.

London embraces me, gently stroking my head. "You don't have to ask, just slide over."

"You both get some rest. I'm going to keep first watch." Melanie says as she leaves the room. I also felt safe with her here. She has been such a help, and been a true friend to the family. She wasn't going far. She had taken us to an abandoned bunker. This particular one had three rooms. A small single bedroom, a bathroom, and a gathering room that had a small area for cooking. There can't be many of these bunkers left.

We lay next to each other all tangled together. I could feel every muscle on his body as he laid next to me, contracting with his every breath. His strength, and his love was the only thing that made me feel totally safe. I felt the stress gradually leave my body as I drifted further and further into unconsciousness. The last thing I hear is London wishing me to sleep well.

Chapter Sixteen

"London, Juniper, wake up! Get up now! It's an emergency!" Melanie screams, jolting us awake. London jumps up, and in seconds he is on his feet as he whips a gun out from under the mattress.

"What th-" I barely get out before London takes over in full protection mode.

"Melanie what's going?" He asks with worry slipping in.

"We've been made. A few enforcers walked passed a little bit ago. Thank radiation that they didn't see the door to this bunker. I took precautions and disguised it earlier. We gotta pack up, and move as quickly as possible. Don't worry about covering up that we were here, we don't have time for that. They'll be back." She says as the three of us get ourselves and our things together.

Fuck, fuck, fuck! They found us! I knew I could never escape her, and she fucking found me! My breathing is becoming erratic, and I can feel my heartbeat in my eyeballs. My body starts to tremble uncontrollably all over the place. I try to calm my breathing, but I fucking can't. Oh shit, not now!

"Fuck! Melanie!"

"What is-Shit!"

I can feel the bed shift as Melanie sits upon it. She grabs

me by the shoulders, forcing me to look at her. "Juniper! You have to fight this! Only you can control your breathing! Please!"

I can see the panic in her eyes, begging me. I'm trying with all of my might, but it seems impossible. I feel the bed shift and see London. He places his hands on either side of my face. I can see the panic in his eyes, but he seems at peace.

"Juniper, I know you're scared. Right now, I think we're all terrified. I want you to close your eyes, and listen to my voice. That's it. I want you to think of our time together. I want you to think of everything we've shared. Are you ready to give that up just yet? Are you ready to give up? If you are, I'll gladly go with you. However, if you're not, I need you to conquer this. I need you to reach deep down into yourself, and become the strong unwavering woman I fell in love with. The woman who doesn't let others make up her mind for her. The woman who takes no shit. The woman who passionately fights for whom she loves. If you're not ready to give in, and you're ready to fight this, then we'll go off together and bring Jaila down.

As he speaks, his words move me. I do not want to give up, and I do not want to have London go down with me. Knowing Jaila, she wouldn't kill us quickly. She'd torture us in front of one another, and she'd kill him in front of me. I won't let that happen, and I won't let my mother's death be in vain. I must snap out of this! I will be the voice of those who've been wrongfully killed. I will bring change to this sorry excuse of an existence. I will not let these past few days be the only moments I've had with London.

I do as he asks, and I focus on our time together. The first time that I saw him, the way he pursued me. I think of the first time we kissed. I think of how he chased after me. I think of how happy I was to see him when he rescued me from Jaila. I think of how I felt when we became one. I think of the pure love we have for each other...

No.

We will not end here.

I stop, opening my eyes, and the trembling ceases. She

will not fucking win. I stare into his eyes for a moment and see his love, and his strength pouring into me. I grab his face and pull it to mine for a quick, but passionate kiss.

"Thank you London. I love you." Melanie was already at the front door. We both grab what we could carry and make our way to her. London stops me just before we reach the door to the bedroom. He pulls me into a deep, but loving hug as he kisses the top of my head. He pulls back just slightly to look at me.

"I love you too." He says his voice thick with emotion. "Alright, let's go." He says, as he releases me and takes hold of my hand. We make our way to Melanie, and see her head pressed against the door listening for the enforcers. She turns to us with panic and resolve written all over her face.

"What is it?"

"London, take her and go through the hidden door under the bed. I will keep them at bay while the two of you escape."

"What?! *No*! You're coming too! No way am I going to leave you behind!"

"There is no time Juniper! Please! Go with London! You, and you alone have to the strength and power to change things. Don't let our sacrifices be in vain."

"Jesus, no! This is all my fault. If I hadn't had a panic attack and slowed us down, you'd be leaving with us! NO! I won't accept this!" I jump towards her to try and grab her, but two strong hands hold me in place. I look up at him in shock. "You can't possibly be okay with this?!"

"When Melanie and I first headed out on this mission, we laid out plans. Then we laid out contingency plans. We were never okay with leaving one of us behind to protect you. We understood that if it came down to it, it would have to be done.."

"NO!!! I will not lose you, or her! Look what they did to me! I will not let you willingly go to that!"

"Melaine... I don't know what to say.."

"London, just promise me that you'll love and protect her. She is our only hope. She is the only one with the strength to do what needs to be done."

"Melanie, it has been an honor to have you as my friend. You have my word."

"Protect her with your life."

"NO NO NO!!!!!! I didn't ask for any of this! I wanted to do this *alone*! I knew something like this was going to happen. I didn't want to get attached! NOOO!"

"Get a grip on yourself! London and I are here because we love you, and chose to be here. You're an exceptional woman Juniper. My only regret is that I will not be able to see what you accomplish."

"No..."

"And who said you get to choose to be alone? Sometimes fate takes control and puts people in your life. I for one am glad that you came into mine." London says, as his grip on me tightens.

"Alright, we're almost out of time. London, Juniper, go!"

I will not let her give herself up! No fucking way. NO FUCKING WAY! I struggle to get out of London's grip. I try and try, but in my condition there is just no hope...

"London, you're going to have to do this for her. I'm so sorry Juniper. There is just no other way."

"London don't you dare! I will never forgive you!" He freezes when I say those words. "I love you, but I will never forgive you if we just leave her here!"

"It hurts me to hear you say those words, but I also know that those words are said in desperation. I told you before I don't like this anymore than you do, but it has to be done."

In that moment, my heart drops. I look at Melanie, fear written all over her. He grabs me, and forces me under the bed. He hits some button under the bed and we drop below. Within minutes after we've fallen into the floor, I hear the enforcers make their way into the room. London hits another button and the wall next to me opens, and he pushes me out. There is only enough room to shimmy out on our backs. He is right behind me, grief stricken.

There are so many things that I want to say to him right

now, but I am stopped in my tracks. I can feel the grief he feels, without him breathing a word. He truly did not want to leave her behind, it's written all over his face and his body.

"Let's go. It's time to move. We don't have much time before they figure out what happened, and we will not let her sacrifice be in vain." No more words were spoken. I followed him as he led the way.

Chapter Seventeen

We ran for hours in silence through dark tunnels. I'd never seen any of them before. London kept looking behind him. I was guessing to make sure I was still there, and that we weren't being followed.

I was still in shock over Melanie. I couldn't believe that we had just left her there... These god damned attacks... I let my fear of Jaila control me. In that moment I let her win.

Never again.

A few more tunnels in, and I felt like I was going to collapse. Every muscle in body was burning. I had to push through it though. I had to make myself keep going. Not for me, but for everyone counting on me. This is for everyone who believed in me, for everyone who has sacrificed for me. Jaila has hurt too many people. Our ancestors did not make it so we could live underground to save the human race, for us to destroy ourselves all over again. If we do, we have nowhere else to run. She is a disease that needs to be wiped out.

"We're almost there Jun, just keep up a little longer." London says to me with his breath short and labored. He has to be at his limit. We both are. The only thing keeping us going at this point is adrenaline.

I try to keep my mind clear and focused on what is

happening right now, but I can't. My mind keeps racing back to when Melanie sacrificed herself so that we could get away.

I just...

It's just not fair. Why must everyone that I love and care about sacrifice so much? I can feel my heart constrict in pain at the knowledge of what is happening to her as we run. This is not fair. This is not fair at all.

I will make it all worth it Melanie. All of the suffering. All of the loss. Jaila and her followers will pay for what they have done, for what they have turned a blind eye to, and what they allowed to happen. London's feet beginning to slow down to a jog took me out of my thoughts.

"Are we close?"

"Just around the next turn. Melanie had me come up with my own backup plan in case this happened. She refused to let me tell her about it in case they got a hold of her and made her talk. She didn't want to risk them having a drug that could make her turn on those she held dear to her." He said it with such sadness that my heart broke even more.

"We're here."

We were stopped in front of a giant metal door.

"London, where are we?" As soon as the words left my mouth, he embraced me in a hug. He held on tight, and I reciprocated in kind. His hands wandered up in my hair, getting tangled in them. He gently moved my head up to meet his lips with mine. It started out slow, but increased with a need. Fast. It's like he was trying to convey all of his feelings in to that kiss, like we may never kiss again. I didn't want to think like that, but I ran with it. I met him with the same passion, and the same feeling. After a few more moments he stopped the kiss, placing his forehead against mine, trying to catch his breath.

"You know I never expected to fall for anyone so quickly, and so fucking hard. They always say once you know, you just know. It will hit you, and there will be nothing that could ever stop you from wanting to be next that person. Wanting to protect that person. Wanting to share everything with that person. And the desire to want them truly and wholly will be so strong, it will drive you mad once you experience it to lose it."

The back of his right hand lightly moves down my cheek as he looks at me with such love. "Lond-." I barely get out above a whisper. He places his pointer finger gently over my lips to silence me as he smiles.

"There is no one else for me. I will fight for you. I will protect you at any cost. I love you Juniper."

I am left standing there speechless. I look at him. I look for the right words to say, but I am drawing a blank. So I do the only thing I can think of that will show him that I feel the same way. I place my hands gently on his face, bringing him in for a sweet, loving, passionate kiss. We stumble backwards until I have him up against the door. I stop the kiss then, not wanting to get too carried away at the risk of being captured. I bring my lips to his ear and whisper, "There is no one else for me either. London, I love you. We're all we've got, and this is all we'll ever need. As long as we have each other, there is nothing we can't do." I say with all the conviction I've got. He looks at me, and his face is full of love.

"Alright, enough of the gushy stuff, we can pick up where we left off once we're safe." He says with that god damned crooked smile. He does that on purpose.

"I need you to trust me." I embrace his hand in mine.

"I'll follow you anywhere."

"Remember that statement. I did some research which lead me to this door. This is one of only two doors that are unknown to the compound."

"Ohh-kayyy? What is the significance?"

"Acting on what you had told me months ago about there being survivors once thrown out of the compound and into the radiation, I searched for old entrances to the compound. Ancient ones. Ancient ones that have been forgotten. I stumbled upon this door in my search for you."

"Are, are you saying that this door leads to surface?!" I asked, my eyes wide in disbelief.

"It is. This is my backup plan. People have been living above ground for a while now. There is no reason to believe that we would drop dead of radiation poisoning once we open the door at the top of the stairs behind this door."

Holy shit... I can't believe he found an unguarded, forgotten entrance to the surface. Can we do this? Can we really make it? Enough with the questions. Enough with the self-doubt. Juniper, pull your head together and go for it. Too many people are counting on you.

"Open the door."

The door makes an unsightly ear piercing screech that I can feel in my teeth. Once through, he closes the door behind him. I look up at him and smile as I take his hand.

"Are you ready Juniper?"

"I'm ready. Whether we die as soon as we open that door, or live and start planning what to do next, I'm glad I'm doing it with you." He smiles at my words and takes a tighter hold on my hand.

Slowly we begin our climb to the top. With each step I remember those who I held most dear, and those whom I loved. I remember those who have sacrificed so that I can be here to make the changes necessary for humans to survive. I need to stop the madness of us living in the underground. With each passing step, the fear of opening the door at the top fades. This is replaced with an unwavering power that I will not stop. I will not stop until I bring her down.

We get to the top. We kiss once more. We place both of our hands on the handle to open it. For the first time in my life, the warm sun hits my face. I take a deep breath as I close my eyes. I open them to London staring at me with love and excitement. We made it! We survived!

Watch out Jaila. We're coming for you next.

JEAN ESTELLE

Epilogue

I'm panicking... I'm fucking panicking! I was asleep when I was woken up by the sirens. Holy fuck! The sirens are so god damn loud!

Oh fuck...

That means...

"Shit!" *I screamed loudly. That means they fucking found us! I turn over to grab her and run. My heart drops to my stomach when I grab nothing but the sheets.*

"JUNIPER?!" *I screamed as my body shook with fear, dread, and panic. How could I not feel her leave? Where the hell did she go?! Why didn't she wake me?! All the months of hiding and always being careful, down the god damn drain. They fucking found us anyway!*

I jumped out of our bed with adrenaline pumping through my body, grabbing the S-34 we have stashed under there for this very fucking reason. I can feel my heartbeat in my ears and the heat on the back of my neck. That is when I hear her scream...

I stare at her in disbelief. I'm unable to comprehend what is happening. My heart was pounding so hard that I could feel each pulse throughout my body. It was true you know, that most people become more aware of their surroundings and small details in times of great stress. I could feel each bead of sweat roll down head, and across my cheekbones. I could hear my own breath stuck in my throat from fear...

I can hear something being dragged. When I whip my head around to see through the bedroom window as they are..

Dragging

Her

Away!

My breath catches in my throat, as all the air leaves my body. I can see the fear in her eyes. All I can think about is how much I love that woman, and how I promised to protect her. I promised keep her safe, to keep those monsters away from her. Here they are putting their grubby little hands on her fucking dragging her away?!

Hell...fucking...no.

Her eyes find mine. They're filled with pain. Fear and pain. When I see that in her eyes, I snap the hell out of it. I can feel the rage boiling up inside of me. The hatred is causing every one of my muscles to tense. I take a deep breath in as I break the glass in the bedroom window. He'll NOT take her! Not as long as there is air in my lungs. I swear with my beating heart, he'll never have her!

Thank you!

Please visit my website for upcoming events, exclusive merchandise, and much more!

Made in the USA
Middletown, DE
08 September 2023

37683537R00097